PRESAGE AND PIRACY

BOW STREET WALLFLOWERS
BOOK THREE

CHERI CHAMPAGNE

Cover design and illustrations by Cheri Champagne. Image inspiration purchased from PeriodImages.com. Interior image design and illustrations by Cheri Champagne.

Editing by Jen Graybeal, My Brother's Editor, and Amanda Bidnall

Logo design and creation by Rachel Champagne

Edition: 1

ISBN: 978-1-7386935-7-3

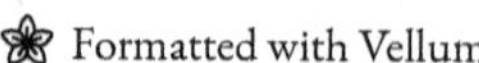 Formatted with Vellum

*For all the badass shes, gays, and theys who fight the good fight
when the shitstorm around you keeps shoving you down.
You've got this.*

CONTENT WARNINGS

Dear reader,

There are certain aspects of this novel that might be triggering to some readers. (Spoilers ahead) They are as follows:

** Mentions of death by fire*
** Mentions of death of parents*
** Forced engagement*
** A lot of cursing*
** Violence*
** Death*
** Mention of traumatic childbirth*
** Choking*
** Murder*
** Poisoning*
** Fat shaming (by villain)*
** Emotional abuse (by villain)*
** Violent battles (hand-to-hand combat, use of blades and pistols)*
** Explicit sex*
** Sex without a condom (without pregnancy)*

PROLOGUE

August 1817

Miss Heather Morgan had timed it perfectly. She'd taken up a spot in a hidden servant's corridor with her squirming sack, waiting for the ideal moment. Her task was to orchestrate a distraction, and that was precisely what she would do.

Once the quadrille was underway, she opened the door leading into the ballroom and emptied the sack.

"*Rats!*" A shrill scream rent the air, followed closely by others.

People moved like a wave along the ballroom floor, everyone shouting or screeching in horror as a plethora of rats bounded heedlessly through the space.

While everyone fled in one direction, Heather went the other, slipping through an opened doorway and into a rear corridor. Maria appeared at the end of the hall, a devilish smirk on her lips.

"Do you think they're sufficiently distracted?" Heather asked breathlessly.

Maria rolled her eyes heavenward as they drew nearer to each other. "We merely required a few minutes' time in order to search the earl's study for the letters."

"We shall have plenty of time, then."

Following the direction the client had given them, they made their way to the study and began to search. They each took one side of the room, testing each drawer and shelf for any hidden compartments. Cordelia would, even now, be searching the earl's bedchamber for the same letters. Lord knew if they would get another chance.

Parchment rustled behind her, and Maria exclaimed, "*Here.* I have them. Do you think that this is all of them?"

"I'll make certain," Heather said, taking the letters and waving a hand at her. "Go on, now! Return to the ballroom and keep everyone busy. I will count the letters and destroy them."

With a nod, Maria swept from the room and returned to the chaos in the ballroom.

"Six, seven...eight," Heather whispered as she counted. The abhorrent letters were all there.

She turned toward the hearth and, for a moment, her heart all but stopped. *Fire.* The orange flames rippled and lapped at the coals, and her heart thudded in her ears. It was so close, the heat from it surrounded her, and the faint screams—

The study door slammed open with a *bang* that reverberated through her chest. Pulse jumping, Heather stared wide-eyed into the furious dark gaze of the Earl of Hanley.

"You *bitch*," he snarled, his lips curling back over yellowing, aged teeth. "I'll tell your aunt about this, Miss Morgan."

This was it, then. The bastard had caught her, knew her family, and had the ability to ruin her life, just as he'd threatened to do to their client. *Well*, she mused, *he'll only ruin life for one of us.*

In one swift movement, she tossed the letters into the fire, the parchment instantly catching ablaze and curling at the ends until it was shrivelled, blackened ash. The tightness in her chest eased a fraction. At least one woman was saved from the man. Now, she merely needed to sort out how to save herself.

The earl's gaze narrowed on her. "I'll see to it that you regret that."

CHAPTER 1

a sennight later

MISERY. Despite the crush of colourful costumes, the strains of a lively quadrille filling the decadent ballroom, and her two closest friends at her side, Miss Heather Morgan's mood had been sucked into a dark hole of despair.

This was her last night in England, and she'd been forced into attending Lord and Lady Ashford's masquerade on the arm of her affianced, Arnold Fitton, the Earl of Hanley. On the morrow, they were to board a navy frigate and sail to the Americas. Heather was being removed from everything she knew and everyone she treasured...including her beloved plants.

It was, however, for good reason.

Once their assignment had been completed and their client released from her entrapment by the "Earl of *Shite*," the man had latched on to Heather to fulfil his apparent duty to his aged cousin in the Americas. He'd not yet given a reason for his urgency to marry—or why, precisely, he required them to wed *in* the Americas—but he was firmly resolved.

Naturally, upon learning of her circumstance, her superior, Miss Grace Huntsbury, and fellow runners had set into action a plan to garner Heather's freedom. Their reconnaissance, however, had unearthed notable scandals and gross transgressions, including—quite possibly—treason.

That was Heather's new assignment: to feign capitulation, journey with the Earl of Shite to the Americas as his affianced bride, and take every opportunity to glean information—and preferably proof—of his dastardly dealings. Once she found what was required, she would make good her escape. And *that* was where her team came in. Percy, their fighting trainer, was already commissioned on board the frigate and would no doubt prove incredibly useful as a man with seafaring knowledge. And Cordelia was to accompany Heather as her maid.

Nervous excitement rippled across her abdomen at the thought of Percy being in such close quarters for such a prolonged period, but she determinedly stifled the feeling. *He is my trainer and a member of my team on this assignment. Pull yourself together, Heather, for pity's sake.*

A bead of perspiration tickled its way down her spine, and she flicked her fan faster.

"Good Lord, it's blistering in here," her friend Maria Sinclair, the new Duchess of Derby, muttered at her side, her fan waving swiftly. "These damned masks don't help, do they?"

"Indeed not," Heather muttered.

The ballroom was sweltering, the opened windows and doors notwithstanding, and the air was choked with the odour of perfume and *people*.

Juliana Notley, the Marchioness of Livingston, nudged Heather's elbow with her own. "I say, Heather, your affianced appears to be in search of you."

Suppressing a groan, Heather peered through the sea of bobbing feather plumes attached to ladies' flagging coiffures, and the plethora of elaborately decorated masks covering the faces of the members of the *haut ton*, and found her husband-to-be. Despite his apparent efforts to dress in costume for the masque, his identity was painfully obvious to those who knew him—which was everyone. Tufts of white hair puffed up around his domino mask, his yellowed teeth stood out against his diaphanous skin, and his belligerent personality was loud and boisterous, even with the chattering around him. And, indeed, his gaze was scanning the ballroom.

"I promised him my waltz," Heather said, her stomach giving a wobble.

Maria covered a mirthful snort with the back of her gloved hand. "The man is simply dreadful. Would that you could complete this assignment here in London rather than venturing off to the Americas."

"Indeed," Heather murmured.

She shook her head, her heavy, beaded mask jostling with the movement. "I confess, now that our departure draws nearer, I'm conflicted. I am eager to begin a new assignment and honoured to take on such a sizeable—and *important*—challenge, yet there is a part of me that mourns a life that I am no longer capable of living."

"That is understandable," Maria put in. "Your life will irrevocably change when you board that frigate."

"And once I return unwed, I shall be ruined," Heather asserted. It was inevitable—and part of their plan—but she could not deny that it stung, even if just a little. "It is fortunate that I have no desire for children, for the burden of my shame would undoubtedly pass to them."

Of course, shame was not the *only* reason she was undesirous to birth children. Two of her mother's sisters had perished in childbirth, and neither had her mother fared well bringing Heather into the world, though she had survived. The thought of birthing a child terrified her. A shiver raced down her spine. Heather's purpose on the planet was far more benevolent and…botanical.

Juliana scowled. "A failing of our society, indeed."

"I imagine children are precisely what the earl desires," Maria added.

Heather grimaced, her stomach roiling at the very notion.

A huff of laughter escaped Juliana as she noted Heather's expression.

"A woman oughtn't be required to provide an heir and spare." Maria frowned.

"But practising is rather fun," Juliana returned.

Her friends laughed, and Heather's abdomen gave another swoop of nerves. Her gaze slid back toward the Earl of Shite, who was wandering aimlessly through the crush. *Tomorrow I leave.*

"You needn't worry, Heather," Juliana began, cutting across Heather's musings. "You've spent enough time training with Percy to sufficiently fend off any unwanted attentions from the earl. And I daresay you shall have plenty of weaponry at your disposal. When I fled home, I had naught but a pistol, a handful of coin, and my mother's jewels. But I—"

"You're the daughter—and the sister—of a duke, Juliana," Heather interjected. "And you nearly died, for pity's sake."

"Only because my cousin wished to kill me."

Heather sighed. "I might only have my assignment with which to contend but, despite how close we are as friends, my life and circumstance differ vastly from both of yours. Juliana, you had a means of escape, and Maria, you… Well, you have the freedom to live multiple lives. My family *watches* me."

Ever since the death of her parents, Heather's aunt and uncle had made no secret of their displeasure of having her in their care, and their distrust of her. She had very little freedom of time—despite what they believed to be her work with charitable causes—no possessions to call her own, and no means to escape. Not to mention her unfashionably red-streaked blonde hair and full figure. It was no wonder her aunt and uncle had leapt at the chance to be rid of her.

Heather heaved another sigh, hating the burst of unease that rippled through her stomach. "Fortunately, once I am ruined, I shall be able to focus more of my time on work, for Grace has generously offered me a room in the Bow Street offices." From there, she could not only continue as a runner but also begin her work as an apothecary.

Another burst of nervous anticipation tingled its way through her middle.

"Oh, yes," Juliana replied with a nod. "Generous, indeed."

There was a beat of silence between them in which the swirling sea of dancers blurred in her vision, and the chatter of conversation, the shuffle of feet, and the clink of champagne flutes dulled behind the pulse whooshing in her ears. She was eager for this assignment, but there was a chance that she would not, in fact, return to London. They all knew it was possible, but no one had yet acknowledged it—mayhap out of fear of casting a pall on their last days together. Or out of hope.

"What of a last night?" Maria asked softly.

A frown puckered Heather's brows beneath her mask. "What happened last night?"

"No," Maria said with a smirk, sending a sideways glance at the slowly advancing earl, then at her husband, and Juliana's, who were in deep conversation but a few steps away. "I mean that you ought to *have* a last night. Lord knows you deserve it, dearest; your bravery is unparallelled. Find a man" —she lowered her voice to a whisper and leaned closer—"with whom to have a tryst before you leave on the morrow. Experience some of the life and excitement that you so desire. Do not let your sojourn to the Americas and potential spinsterhood dampen what might very well be a fine evening. It shall provide you with a boost of courage."

"A man?" Heather scoffed. She hadn't considered the option, but it did appeal. "As much as I might like the notion of having some man—*any* man—before my perilous assignment and impending ruination, how am I to find such a someone? I'm a wallflower, Maria. Or have you forgotten? No man has so much as glanced at me in years."

"I daresay any man would fall into your bed with little to no provocation, Heather," Juliana put in. "Men are... predictable in that way. All you must do is show them a little interest—"

"And some bosom." Maria nodded.

"And then, with a flirt and a smile, I'm certain you'll have your man."

It *was* her last night in England, for Lord knew how long. Perhaps if she skirted the card room, she could catch a man's eye. Another droplet of perspiration tickled the space between her breasts, and she resisted the urge to scratch at it. Mayhap she ought to seek solace on the terrace and cool down.

"There you are, my dear," the earl boomed with false joviality. He shoved his elbow toward her. "I believe this dance is ours."

With an internal squaring of her shoulders, Heather nodded to her friends, pasted a false smile on her lips, and accepted his proffered arm. The strains of a waltz filled the ballroom, and determination swelled in her chest.

They took up their positions among the other dancers, and she allowed him to lead her in a perfectly dreary waltz. His hot, fetid breath wafted over to her and, in an effort to avert her nose from the offending odour, she tilted her face toward the other dancers.

As distressing as the evening was, the ballroom was rather

splendid. The floor and columns were swirled white-and-grey marble, the walls white-painted wood panelling, the ceiling artfully arched and trimmed with gilt that spread to every column and balustrade, including the orchestra's balcony. It was marvellous. But bloody hot. And overwhelming with offending odours. *And fire.*

Her gaze slipped over the delicate chandeliers—and the candles gracing them—and she suppressed a shiver.

The earl spun her in a turn and squeezed her hand tighter, diverting her attention back to her assignment. She pasted a vapid smile on her lips. The man believed her to be capitulating to a marriage due to his threat of ruination—which would occur regardless—while in actuality, *she* was the one in control. She was, in a very real sense, acting as a spy.

"Would that you had chosen something brighter to don than...*this*," he muttered. "You look like a widow."

"This is a masquerade," she returned, though she fully acknowledged that she'd chosen black as an act of protest against her engagement to the dreadful man. "I am a raven."

"I know what you're doing." His voice dipped to an angry murmur, his breath hot on her cheek. "But I shan't be deterred. You are now mine, regardless of your little rebellion. Tomorrow, our adventure begins. I've paid handsomely for our passage. We shall both have officers' cabins—"

"Are those not meant for the officers?" she asked pertly.

His hand tightened again, and his blue eyes hardened behind his domino. "You're welcome to sleep in a hammock among the crew."

Bastard. "I'll take the cabin, thank you."

"Ah." He forced a wide smile. "Excellent choice."

Heather feigned idle curiosity and boldly inquired, "Why are we to journey upon a navy frigate and not—"

He scoffed, his shoulders drawing back to puff out his chest in arrogance. "As an orphan of no means, I forgive your ignorance. *I*, however, am an earl with high connections. I spoke to one *exceedingly* prominent royal on the matter of our journey, and he most generously offered his support. The captain of the frigate will do anything I demand."

Curiosity piqued, Heather feigned only mild interest as the earl continued to boast. What royal could have agreed to align himself with the Earl of Shite? And was that royal aware of this man's potentially traitorous dealings?

The earl's grip on her tightened painfully as the last notes of the waltz hung in the air, effectively drawing her attention back to him.

His jaw tightened in a maniacal smile as he leaned close to press his lips to her ear. "You'll do as you're told on this journey, Calluna, or you shall face my wrath."

Heather hid a cringe at his use of her given name. Her parents had been devoted in their study of horticulture—very much like Heather herself—and had named their only child after their favourite flower: *Calluna Vulgaris*—Heather.

She could only surmise the Earl of Shite chose to use *Calluna* over her preferred name, *Heather*, because he knew it bothered her. And it did. Though likely not for the reason he presumed. Indeed, she adored her name—when her parents had used it. This blackguard was defiling it.

She nodded, and he retreated, his malevolent gaze locking onto hers with intended meaning. Heather lowered her gaze in an effort to appear sufficiently cowed. The man, however, had only served to strengthen her resolve.

Her friends were correct: she couldn't leave on the morrow without first experiencing something that would be *hers*. It was precisely the boost of confidence she required.

But how to choose a man? And, her friends' advice aside, how could she be certain that the man would be interested?

"PLEASE EXPLAIN why you brought me here tonight," Percy Baxter muttered to his friend and former employer, Leonard Notley, the Marquess of Livingston, his gaze dispassionately scanning the throng of bedecked dancers.

"My wife and her friends wished to come." Leo scratched at his chin absently. "They're acquaintances and, dare I say, friends of yours now as well. I thought you would enjoy yourself. It is your last night in London for some time, after all."

Despite his prior comfort on the open sea, a jolt of nervousness tightened his insides. "Miss Grace Huntsbury is my new *employer*, and the other young women are my *protégées*. I would scarcely call them friends, regardless of how affable they might be."

"And pretty?" Leo lifted a golden eyebrow.

A flash of red-streaked blonde hair, a full figure, and a challenging smirk raced across his mind's eye, but he glared at his friend. "I know what you are attempting to do, Leo, and it shan't work."

Leo hummed, his gaze dark behind his domino as he swallowed a gulp of champagne.

"I might have been a...well, you know what I used to be," Percy muttered, "but I'm not a cad, for Christ's sake. I'll not besmirch a gentlewoman's name—nor her bloodline—by forcing my attentions on her. While I'm away, my duties are clear: I shall be a protector and support for Heather—nothing more."

"Come, now." Leonard sipped at his champagne once more. "You've plenty to offer a gentlewoman. I daresay—"

"These people are toffs, Leo," Percy grumbled. "I don't belong here. Hell, at one time, *neither* of us would have belonged here. Look at me." He tugged at the hem of his outrageously purple waistcoat and feather-adorned coat. "I look like a sodding peacock."

"Half the men here look like sodding peacocks," Leo replied. "It's a *masque*."

Percy rolled his eyes.

"But you belong here just as much as anyone else, Percy," Leonard continued. "You've earned your place, to be sure."

With a shake of his head, Percy bit the inside of his lips and let the argument go. Leo would never know what it felt like to be a true outsider, for while he might have been a man of the sea at one time, he was born a gentleman. Percy was not.

His stomach twisted again at the reminder of where he would be on the morrow. And the restlessness itching beneath Percy's skin only worsened as they stood observing the dancers. He needed a good release.

Accepting a flute of champagne from atop the tray of a passing footman, Percy gulped it back. He wasn't a man to philander or prey on women, and he hadn't any intention to become one. He'd never truly been in want of company long. Someone always approached *him*.

His gaze scanned the crush of elaborately costumed gentry. *These* women, however, were not for him.

"It's damned hot in here," Leonard grumbled.

Percy grunted his agreement. It was, indeed.

The lilting music came to a stop, and the dancers bowed and curtseyed politely to one another before leaving the dance floor.

"I'm going to seek out Juliana's hand in a quadrille," Leo said. "Will you be well here?"

Percy notched his chin. "Of course. Go on and make your wife happy. I might take a walk."

CHAPTER 2

The hum of music and chattering voices faded as Heather made her way across the terrace. The sweet fragrance of late spring flowers carried on the breeze that cooled her heated skin. She padded on slippered feet to the waist-high granite railing and gazed up at the dark sky.

It was a pity that one couldn't see the stars when in town. More was the pity that she might never lament the loss again, for she mightn't ever return to London.

Her stomach swooped, and her chest tightened, but she swiftly dismissed the thought as ludicrous. In the past week, she and Percy had trained relentlessly in combat, enough that she felt confident in her ability to defend herself should the need arise.

Truthfully, it was the loss of her plants that she mourned. After much debate, the earl had capitulated and had given her permission to bring several of her plants aboard the ship. But it wasn't enough. It would never be enough.

She rounded the railing and stepped onto the garden path, letting the fragrance of the flowers lure her. The voices and music faded entirely, leaving just her own footsteps on the gravelled path and a gentle breeze to fill her ears.

When her parents had passed, Heather had inherited numerous plants—in various states of germination—from their studies in botany. And while her dear friend Juliana had promised to keep the remainder of Heather's plants safe at Woodhaven Hall, where her new husband had remarkable conservatories, it neither brought Heather joy nor sufficiently eased her mind. Or her heart. Since her parents' death, her plants, her friends, and her aspirations on Bow Street were the only things that brought meaning to her life.

In the event of an emergency, many of her plants would prove useful, but predicting those emergencies, and knowing which ones to bring with her, had proven difficult. From what little she'd already learned, some of her plants could provide nourishment while others could treat wounds, but she didn't yet know enough of the practice of an apothecary to determine which was which.

Prior to being ensnared by the Earl of Shite and taking on her significant assignment, she'd hoped to broaden her collection of plants, with the specific intention of providing healing herbs, tinctures, and whatnot to the women of Bow Street. She had fully intended to become their permanent provider of medicinal plants—dried or fresh, as required.

For now, however, and despite the ache it put in her heart, she would turn her focus to uncovering proof of the earl's iniquitous dealings.

Stopping in her tracks, Heather touched her fingertips to the bud of a pink rose.

"It's a lovely evening," a deep, rumbling growl said from behind her.

Heather spun, her heart in her throat and her body poised for attack, staring through the obscurity at a man...dressed as a peacock.

Amusement relaxed her tense muscles. Feathers stuck out at all angles from his coat, and the purple of his waistcoat seemed somehow bright under the moon's hazy glow. There, however, was where the ridiculousness of his costume ended. His legs were thick and muscular, his shoulders impossibly broad, and his neck—*blimey*—his neck had incredible girth. Gloved hands double the size of hers hung at his sides, and his eyes glittered darkly behind his domino. Beneath the mask, his lips were full, and quirked up in a cocksure grin as though the man knew precisely how his visage made women feel.

Even obscured by the darkness of night, this man was a sight. She knew large men—Percy, for example was particularly large—but, despite the plumage, this man cut a dashing figure that made her breath quicken.

"I did not hear you approach, sir," she said breathily.

His smile grew, revealing gleaming white teeth. "My apologies for startling you, madam."

"What are you doing out in the gardens?" *Foolish question, Heather.*

"Going for a walk. Escaping the heat of the ballroom," he whispered. His gaze swept over her, from the tips of the black ribbons in her hair to the hem of her black, feather-adorned dress. "You?"

Her breath caught in her throat at the flare of heat in his dark gaze. Her friends had been right on that score—she *did* know that this man was interested. "The same."

"You ventured into the gardens *alone*?" His voice was a breathy growl.

"Yes," she replied on a gasp. *For pity's sake, Heather, pull yourself together!*

Tingles prickled along her skin as she took in the man's relaxed stance. There was no doubt in her mind that he would give her the last night she so desired and boost her confidence before her assignment.

She boldly took a step closer to him as the wind ruffled the feathers upon his coat and carried his impossible scent to her. Absurdly, she imagined that he smelled of salt—like the ocean's spray—and soap. It was intriguing, alluring...and achingly familiar.

She stepped yet nearer, and his gaze darkened on hers. It became more evident the closer she drew just how very tall the man was. Despite her own substantial height, her forehead scarcely reached his chin.

Who *was* this man? Part of her was desirous to peek beneath his domino, but there was something decidedly thrilling about an anonymous flirtation.

A delicious heat melted low in her belly. He was so close she could feel the warmth radiating off his body.

Blimey, but they had scarcely exchanged a few words in the dark and she was fully prepared to give him her virtue. In fact, *she* was attempting to seduce *him*.

PERCY'S PULSE fluttered in his chest, his every nerve attuned to the mysterious woman's movements and his stiffening cock wedged firmly between his thigh and his too-tight breeches. The woman stirred the scent of flowers around her as she approached, their bodies very nearly touching.

Christ, but she was skilled at seduction. And Percy was eager to be seduced. The daringly low-cut bodice, long black silk gloves, and matching feathered frock told him that she was a widow—a young one, at that—and likely well-versed in the art of the tryst. That was a relief, for he couldn't taint a woman's reputation with his name. But a widow of middling reputation—fuck knows a *lady* wouldn't venture out into the gardens alone—understood the way of society and the risks involved in a tryst.

"Does your wife await your presence in the ballroom?" she asked coyly.

He shook his head in one swift movement. "I'm unattached."

A low, purring hum sounded from deep in her throat, and Percy's cods tightened.

Her hair, of indeterminate colour, waved in the breeze, catching the moon's hazy glow. Another flash of a challenging gaze and a thick, shapely form raced through his mind's eye, and his shoulders stiffened. It was dark, but from what he could see of this woman, she carried herself like one who'd experienced much of the world—and had a similar physique to a certain student of his who had been inappropriately occupying his thoughts of late. It would be wise, in this instance, to take this widow up on her offer, for evidently it had been too long.

"What is your name?" Percy blurted, his voice far lower than he recognised.

The widow's full lips widened, and eyes of indistinguishable colour gleamed with mischief behind her mask.

"Ah-ah," she chided on a whisper. "You mustn't break the rules of the masque."

He matched her grin and murmured, "You follow the rules, do you, madam?"

Her gaze burned into his as she inched closer. "The rules of the masque, indeed, must always be followed. However"—she hesitated, and his heart faltered—"the rules of society? Most assuredly not."

A groan escaped him, unbidden. "A woman after my own heart."

With a gloved hand, she reached up to touch one of the ridiculous peacock feathers that adorned his coat, her gaze heated. "And what if I desire something other than your heart?"

He cursed under his breath. Whatever this woman wanted, it was hers.

Her words were so soft, Percy strained his ears to hear over the rush of his own pulse.

"Kiss me."

Without another word, Percy swept down and captured her lips with his. At the very back of his mind, he was dimly aware of their masks knocking together, but his attention was narrowed onto the feel of her and—*Christ*—his body's reaction.

Lips as soft as the petals of a flower parted beneath his, her tongue matching his movements with tentative, explorative flicks. She tasted like champagne, flowers, and sin. And he bloody loved it. His cock throbbed, painfully hard against his hip, and his stomach buzzed with anticipation.

Percy was Achilles, and this widow was his heel. He was utterly helpless in the face of such intense longing.

Voices sounded from the terrace, and, with regret, Percy drew back. Without breaking their gaze, he touched the tips of his callused fingers to her jaw, and a shiver wracked her frame.

"Would you care to join me for a stroll deeper into the gardens?" The question was innocent enough, but his voice was thick with arousal.

"The gazebo," she breathed.

He linked her hand around his elbow and led her down the garden's path. The thrum of anticipation and desire beneath his skin was like banked coals, hot and ready to ignite.

They wove between the flowerbeds and shrubberies, making their way through the darkness. The air was cool against his heated skin, and the gravelled path crunched beneath their feet.

Heart thumping madly, he scanned the shadows, ensuring their solitude before drawing her within. The gazebo glowed milky white in the moonlight, and despite its shrouded interior, his eyes adjusted swiftly. The fragrance of flowers followed them inside.

His senses were alive. Hell, but it had been far too long since he'd had a woman.

HEATHER'S EYES quickly adjusted to the darkness, her breath hitching at the man's sheer size. He was but a shadow in the space, but he loomed large. Before taking a position on Bow Street and beginning her training, Heather might have found such a man intimidating. Now, however, she knew at least seven ways in which to fell him should he attempt to do her harm.

At the moment, all she felt was eagerness and desire.

The shutters surrounding the gazebo were closed, creating a private circular space bordered by a bench that appeared to be covered with pillows. An ideal place for a tryst.

Oh, hell. Am I really doing this?

The man's breath still came fast, a clear sign of his excitement, and her core gave a responding throb. She wanted this.

"We haven't much time," she said, her voice husky and entirely foreign to her ears.

He nodded once and tore his coat from his shoulders, then went to work on his waistcoat buttons and cravat. Heather followed his lead and removed her gloves, then went to work on her feathered costume.

"Allow me," he said hoarsely.

She turned her back to him, and he nimbly unbuttoned the black frock, helped her step from it, and draped it carefully over the edge of the circular bench. He reached for the ties of her corset, but she stayed him.

"We needn't bother with those." In the interest of saving time, keeping layers on was paramount. Additionally, she felt absurdly conscious of her naked body being on display for this unknown man. While she was by no means uncomfortable with her size or weight—no matter what her aunt and cousins said—the thought of such vulnerability, in a moment when she wished to be strong, rankled. This was a moment she was taking for herself.

He gave a sharp nod and pulled his shirt over his head, careful not to dislodge his silk domino mask. And she gasped, long and loud in the small space. While he was still in shadow, her eyes had adjusted enough for her to discern his marvellous —and utterly fascinating—body.

From his narrow waist, up his muscular abdomen and broad chest, and down his thick arms, the man was almost entirely covered with images. The expanse of his chest was covered with a large image of an anchor with rope woven around it, and surrounding it were images of swallows in flight. She couldn't discern their colours, or the images that graced his arms, but that anchor... *Blimey*.

Almost instantly, a wave of uncertainty tightened his muscles and thinned his lips. *Drat*. She'd been staring too long. If she had more time, she would dedicate it to thoughtfully exploring every inch of his torso. But she had an elderly earl to return to before he came in search of her.

So, before the mysterious man could turn away, she reached out. "May I touch you?" she whispered.

His throat bobbed before he said gutturally, "*Christ*, yes."

With a small smile and her stomach abuzz with nerves, she pressed her hands firmly to his abdomen. His skin was hot to the touch, but also markedly soft. She palmed a path over his broad chest and shoulders and down his muscular arms. *Law*, but the man was afire, his body both hard and soft simultaneously.

With that touch, the moment changed. He dipped to take

her lips with his. Their masks bumped, and Heather relished the restriction, the mystery.

His tongue flicked erotically over hers, each movement eliciting tingles of excitement throughout her body. A moan escaped her, and she clutched his shoulders tighter as he ground his hips against hers. The hard ridge of his erection rubbed deliciously against her cleft.

Something about the man was comforting—*familiar*—as though her body had known the touch of him before. It was impossible, of course, but the feeling calmed what few nerves she had about the encounter.

"I want you," she breathed.

He groaned and broke their kiss to trail his lips along the side of her neck, his arms coming around her waist and pulling her against him.

"I have but one stipulation," she continued on a whisper.

Body stilling, he drew back to look her in the eyes. "Of course."

Heather hesitated, a blush creeping over her cheeks. She'd heard enough of her friends' encounters—and had read a great deal on the subject—to know what she wanted. But dare she confess her desire? She desperately wanted to remember this moment, to have it burned into her memory, sustaining her for the remainder of her life after she was removed from society. *Yes.* She must. "Don't be gentle."

A low, rumbling growl vibrated in his chest. "As you desire."

In a blur of activity, the mysterious man had her sitting on the edge of the gazebo's perimeter bench, pillows at her back. He threw one to the ground and shockingly lowered himself to his knees before her.

"I need to see you," he growled.

With sure movements, he tugged at the low neckline of

her chemise and popped one breast out above her corset. Another rumble came from his chest.

"So pert and pink." Wrapping one arm between her back and the pillows, he held her close and took the nipple into his mouth.

A hot burst of pleasure swept her from head to foot as he teased. His tongue flicked, his teeth scraped, and—*good God*—the suckling! Her hands drifted to his hair, careful to not dislodge the ties of his domino as he lavished her breast with attention.

He swiftly exposed the other and repeated his attentions, garnering breathy moans from her.

She wanted this man without question.

Rather suddenly, he pulled back to bunch her skirts around her abdomen, his gaze locked on her exposed cunny. Her stomach gave a swoop of giddy nerves. His callused hands rubbed along her inner thighs, massaging the muscles, and her pulse skipped. A delectable quivering began low in her belly, the sensation preceding a wanton throbbing through her core.

Then her mind was rendered entirely blank as his head disappeared between her legs and he licked her cleft. Pleasure shot through her, and a keening moan was pulled from her lips.

He grunted again, the heat of his breath against her cunny adding to her excitement. He laved in earnest, consuming her with erotic strokes of his tongue.

Unable to keep her hands to herself, she reached down to grip his hair in her fists as he worked, flicking over each sensitive nerve, and—*oh*, the gentle suction from his lips!

She knew of the "little death" from her friends and could recognize the impending rupture in the tightening of her muscles, the stuttering of her breath...and the utterly delectable tingling that rippled through her in ever-strengthening waves.

"*My God*," she whimpered. "*I'm going to—*"

With a ragged gasp, he drew back. "I need to be inside you when you come," he ground out.

Heather groaned, already missing his touch.

His lips quirked. "I haven't any condoms. Have you taken precautions?"

Her mind awhirl with lust, Heather blinked at the man. *Condom? Precautions?* She'd never heard of the former, but she was not too lust-addled to mistake his meaning. He wished to know if she had any protection against pregnancy.

"No," she blurted.

He nodded, and with a heated glance, he unfastened his breeches and slid them down in one smooth motion. She had a mere moment to take in his enormous, ruddy, jutting erection before he gripped it and slid the tip of himself against her.

Sparks danced behind her eyelids at the contact.

"*Oh*," she breathed.

He used her damp arousal as a means to lubricate his member before he pressed himself inside. The muscles in his arms and shoulders tensed as he gripped her hips in his large hands and thrust hard, breaking through her maidenhead and filling her fully in one swift move.

She hid a grimace at the pinch of pain, and her husky gasp mingled with the mystery man's panting. While the pain had been minimal, she felt so...*full*.

Then he began to move. Withdrawing, then thrusting deep inside her again and again, the build-up of pleasure mounted once more. Widening her thighs, she shifted her pelvis until, with every thrust of his hips, he wrought the most delicious pleasure. She traced her hands over every inch of his skin within her reach, relishing the quiver of his muscles beneath her touch.

"*Christ*," he gasped. "You're so...tight. You feel...so good."

"As do you," she replied truthfully.

Heat coiled around her once more, but there was something missing. Her climax was just out of her reach.

Groaning, he released one of her hips and pressed a thumb into her labia, swiftly finding the pearl of pleasure.

"*Yes*," she urged.

He swirled his thumb around her cleft, the friction adding just what she needed to reach her—

Blinding light burst behind her eyelids. Back arching, her breath stuttered, and her body tensed in a paroxysm of ecstasy.

"*Fuck*," the man cursed, his dark eyes hot on her through his domino.

His hips pumped feverishly, the friction only prolonging the torrent of her gratification.

All at once, he withdrew, his spine stiffened, his teeth bared themselves on a snarl, and his skin flushed as his seed spilled in hot spurts on her inner thigh.

CHAPTER 3

Heart thundering madly in his chest, Percy struggled to catch his breath after a climax that had rocked him to his toes. Hell, but the woman was tight and responsive. Her every throaty moan and gasp had his ballocks tightening.

She smiled at him, her teeth gleaming in the darkness beneath her mask. "You're markedly skilled at that."

He tucked himself back into his breeches. Percy wouldn't call himself skilled at sex, but that had been...remarkably good. "Mayhap we bring out the best in each other."

Now, however, wasn't the time to think too deeply on it. She'd been correct earlier: they hadn't much time.

With a flick of his wrist, he withdrew a handkerchief from the inner pocket of his discarded coat and gave the woman a cursory wipe before he tossed the cloth aside.

Despite his bewildering desire to remain sequestered in the gazebo with this widow, he stood, fixed her skirts, and helped her to her feet. Their re-dressing was swift and silent, but he could swear that her cries of pleasure still rang in his ears. He straightened his cravat and tugged on his ridiculously feathered coat-sleeves, then helped the woman fasten her gown—all while the scent of flowers and their coupling filled his senses.

Unable to resist the pull of the woman, Percy stepped close and wrapped his arms around her waist. "Thank you." He pressed a lingering kiss to her lips, letting his tongue play leisurely with hers now that the heat of passion had subsided.

They broke apart with a gasp. "Thank *you*," she breathed.

"Come," he said softly, offering his arm. "I shall return you to the terrace."

She nodded, her colour still high as she accepted his proffered arm and walked with him from the gazebo.

The air had grown cooler since they'd entered, the breeze ruffling the feathers on their costumes and the wisps of the woman's hair.

Damn, but he wished he knew who the widow was, for he would definitely seek her out again—once he returned from his assignment, of course. He caught her gaze through the dim moonlight, his chest constricting. "Won't you tell me your name?"

Her lips curved in a half smile before she lifted on her toes to press a soft kiss to his cheek. "Good night."

With that, she disappeared across the terrace and through the opened doors to the ballroom.

Percy blinked at her retreating figure, his heart and thoughts oddly unable to comprehend what had just occurred. To his confusion, a tingling nervous sensation travelled up and down each of his limbs. It had all happened so quickly that, if not for his sense of being utterly replete, he might have thought their encounter a dream.

His feet moved, the clipped sound of his footfalls filling his ears before he, too, reached the ballroom. Hot, stuffy air hit him as he entered, but his feet continued to drive him forward.

He scanned the masked faces and costumes, looking for any sign of the mysterious woman, an unfamiliar hum vibrating through him at the prospect of spotting her through the throng. Fans waved and dancers swept past, and, despite himself, Percy's lungs deflated in defeat. She'd made it clear that she didn't want him to know her name until the unmasking. Perhaps she didn't wish for him to know her *at all*. Certainly she'd enjoyed herself, but might she be the sort of woman who wished for only a tryst and not a protector? If so, he ought to respect her wishes—most particularly because he was to leave London on the morrow.

"Why so glum?" Leonard asked, sauntering to his side. "You disappeared for some time. Did something unpleasant occur?"

"Quite the contrary, I assure you," Percy muttered.

"Indeed?" His friend's eyes brightened behind his domino.

Percy inclined his head. "I met a woman."

"Ah." Leo nodded in understanding. "In the gardens?"

"Gazebo."

Leo gestured suggestively with one hand. "And were both parties...*pleased* with the interaction?"

"Quite."

"Then..." Leo left the question unvoiced, and Percy sighed.

"I wanted more."

"Ah, yes. I see."

"Rather."

Leo sucked at his teeth. "And do you know the woman's name?"

"No," Percy grunted. "And I daresay I wouldn't recognize her voice—even should I hear it again—for she whispered nearly every word."

"No chance for a repeat encounter, then."

"I should say not."

The strains of another quadrille echoed through the grand

room, and Leonard clapped Percy on the back. "Chin up, Percy."

"Capital advice. Thank you."

HEATHER SLIPPED into the corridor alongside the ballroom and found her way to the ladies' retirement room. Despite the mystery man's efforts, her inner thighs felt decidedly damp and in need of a more thorough cleaning. Law, but it was a messy business, this *making love*. But decidedly worth the mess.

"Is anyone here?" she murmured into the small room just off the corridor. When no reply was forthcoming from beyond the privacy screen that hid the chamber pots from view, she entered and locked the door behind her.

In an effort at efficiency and expediency, she poured water from a pitcher into one of the two washbasins atop a low chest of drawers and plunged a cloth into the chilled depths. She wrung the cloth, then lifted her skirts, carefully wiping away the faint smears of her blood and a splotch of a slick, milky substance that she could only assume was the man's seed.

Her stomach dipped, and she hastily rinsed the cloth, then deposited the water out the window before she left, effectively discarding all evidence of her tryst.

The heat from the ballroom was suffocating, but Heather wove her way through the crush of masked patrons, her heart and mind entirely at odds with her surroundings. She'd successfully changed her life in a matter of minutes. *She*, Heather Morgan—the woman with no parents, few friends, and fewer prospects, who'd been forced into an engagement with an extortionist had done something with her own life. And she had loved every moment of it.

"There you are," Maria said, leaving a group of admirers

and approaching through the crush. "I haven't seen you in an age. Where did you get off to?"

Heather's stomach dipped again, her nerves bubbling just beneath her skin. She glanced around in search of prying ears, and whispered, "I had a *last night*."

Maria's eyes widened behind her mask. "My god, Heather! Did you *really*?"

"I did. In the gazebo."

Her friend slapped a hand over her mouth to suppress her laugh of surprise before she leaned in conspiratorially. "Who was it?"

Heather shook her head, dislodging a lock of her red-blonde hair. "I don't know."

Maria gasped. "You had a—" She lowered her voice and leaned yet closer. "You had an anonymous tryst with someone? Was he a guest?"

"Yes, I believe so. He was in costume—dressed as a peacock."

Her friend's gaze snapped past Heather to scan the dancers. "There are dozens of peacocks here this evening. Which one is *your* peacock?"

Heather followed Maria's gaze into the dizzying array of costumes. "He was a large man, thick, muscularly built...but I'm afraid that I did not see him well enough in the darkness to pick him out in—"

"You didn't get a good look?" Maria said disbelievingly. "You mean to say that you didn't look at *it*?"

Heat flared in Heather's cheeks, and she clucked her tongue. "I saw *it*, but I daresay I cannot expect to examine every cock in the ballroom to identify the man."

"Who's examining cocks?" Juliana asked furtively, joining them from Maria's other side.

"Heather took our advice," Maria said with a grin and a wicked gleam in her eye.

"Excellent." Juliana beamed. "Who was the man with the good fortune to capture our dear friend's attention?"

"It was *anonymous*," Maria hissed.

Heather sighed. "He was magnificent, though. Large and skilled."

"And you took precautions?" Juliana asked.

"To prevent getting with child?" Maria added in a whisper.

"We did, yes," Heather returned. "Despite my adoration for children, I'm not the right sort to be a mother."

"We know, dearest," Maria said with a soft smile.

Heather sighed.

The earl no doubt expected to sire a child directly upon their arrival in the Americas. She must, therefore, accomplish her task before they reached the other shore.

"Ah." A familiar—dreaded—voice came from behind her. "My dear Calluna."

"Lord Hanley, how lovely to see you again." Maria dipped in a shallow curtsey.

He bowed in return, his thin white hair waving over his domino at the movement. "Your Grace." The old man extended his elbow to Heather. "I believe that the last waltz of the evening is upon us! Come along now."

Heather's pulse hiccoughed with a combination of sorrow and worry, while her stomach buzzed with hope and eagerness over her assignment. She offered the man a small smile as she took his proffered arm and allowed him to lead her into her final waltz in London.

A WAVE of possessiveness washed over Arnold Fitton, the Earl of Hanley, as he gripped his future bride's arm and led her to the dance floor.

That's right, men, this one's mine.

The wench wasn't the young lady he'd first intended to ensnare as a means to fulfil his cousin's demands, but after she had burned the documents tying him to his previous intended, he hadn't another choice. Threatening her, her family, and her friends with ruination had been more than enough to garner her hand. Foolish lamb.

Of course, her family was eager to be rid of her—and no wonder, with that garish, red-tinged hair and corpulent figure. Her tits were adequate, he would grant, but they added little to her appeal. She was, however, *his,* and would do well enough to satisfy his dying cousin and earn the entailment he'd been promised.

Arnold gritted his teeth. Christ knew why his blackguard of a cousin's estate wasn't already entailed to the man to whom the title would pass—mayhap laws were different in the Americas—but Arnold would see to it that he was given what he was owed.

Calluna was precisely what was required. He would marry the wench in front of his cousin, gain the man's fortune, land, and title after his imminent demise, and return to England with wealth and a whelp.

CHAMPAGNE BUBBLED down Percy's throat as he scanned the ballroom. Music lilted through the space, the energy high and the air pregnant with anticipation. Dancers swirled and twirled, the majority of those in attendance participating in at least this last dance. But not Percy. He, like the wallflowers and chaperones of the evening, stood at the perimeter of the ballroom and observed.

He swallowed another gulp of champagne, his gaze searching for a black, feathered gown and artfully styled—if wind-swept—chignon with black ribbons. Despite himself, curiosity ate at him. Even if the woman had no desire to continue a flirtation, and he was bound for the Americas on the morrow, the urge to at least see her face burned through him.

Dancers whirled past him in pinks, blues, reds, greens... A flash of black feathers caught his gaze, and his spine stiffened. Could it be?

His pulse quickened with interest.

But no. That woman had a toppling chignon of brown hair spotted with pearls.

Disappointment slammed through him, but he kept his gaze moving. Far too many women had donned black that evening, curse it. *There!* Blonde-red hair with black ribbons. He strained his neck but failed to garner a clear view of her costume. She danced with a vaguely familiar older man with a halo of stringy white hair.

The music swelled and the dancers spun, but Percy kept his gaze locked on the mystery widow. His pulse sped faster, his breath quickening with anticipation as the waltz came to a close and the dancers clapped. He was distantly aware of someone speaking from the musicians' balcony, but the sound was muted by the rush of blood in his ears. *The unmasking.*

He hastily shuffled sideways, tilting his head in an effort to garner a better view of the bewitching widow. *There!* His pulse rushed in his ears, muting the hum of anticipation in the room. Her hands delicately swathed in her elbow-length black gloves, the woman reached up to untie her mask.

The mask fell away to reveal her face...and his blood froze solid in his veins.

My god. His gut twisted painfully, and an icy dread dampened his skin. It couldn't be. It simply *couldn't*. Heather Morgan—his *student*, for fuck's sake! She was to be married, was leaving for the Americas on the morrow. She was on assignment...with Percy.

Miss Morgan joined in the applause and pasted on a patently false smile for her intended before Leo, Jasper, and their wives encircled her and the Earl of Hanley. They chatted amiably for a moment, and Percy watched as though glued to his spot.

What have I done?

Nervous energy bubbled inside him, and he had to move. Without a backward glance, he wove through the milling guests, down the corridor, across the foyer, and through the front door. He ignored the waiting footmen and coachmen and strode directly for the street, needing desperately to clear his head.

The clip of his boots on the cobblestones echoed around him, and the oil lamps lent a dim light.

Heather Morgan. Hell, but he ought to have known it was her. He'd even compared the "widow's" hair and figure to Heather's, for fuck's sake. He'd been wilfully ignorant. *Hell's teeth.* His gut gave another hard twist as guilt churned through him. She was very likely an innocent, and he'd just robbed her of her maidenhead. *Fuck.*

In the heat of the moment, he'd thought her a widow well versed in the art of the tryst. He'd assumed she knew herself and the risks involved. While he'd withdrawn when he'd spilled his seed, that did not guarantee that she would not get with child—or so he'd learned from acquaintances with troubled mistresses.

He sighed, and shook his head. Society mothers were notorious for ill-informing their daughters about relations between men and women, instead hoping that their future husbands would take care of it. But Heather's mother had passed some time ago, and she was not yet married... It was possible her aunt had spoken with her, but from what Percy had gleaned about the woman, that was unlikely.

He reached up to pinch the bridge of his nose, but was impeded by his curst domino. Agitation rode him, and he tugged the thing from his head and shoved it into his pocket.

"*Fuck*," he growled into the darkness.

It was fortunate he was already assigned to the frigate alongside Heather, for his duty was clear. Naturally, he understood her reasoning behind the tryst—she would be ruined upon their return, after all—but it begged the question: had she known it was *him* behind the mask?

CHAPTER 4

"Will you just tell me what happened?" Leo pleaded, watching from the chaise longue as Percy paced before the hearth.

Percy rubbed a hand over his drawn features and scrubbed at his dry eyes. After preparing a small satchel of items and paying his future months' rent for his bachelor's apartments, he'd spent hours through the night staring at his ceiling and replaying the tryst in his mind.

Guilt hit him square in the gut once more, and he spun in another turn to pace back before the hearth.

He'd only just recently acquired the rooms above a shop, near enough to walk to his new post as an instructor for the women of Bow Street. The women were quick to learn under his tutelage and would do well with his superior—Grace Huntsbury—while he and Heather were away.

"Does it call to you once more?" Leo asked, his voice low and tinged with concern.

Percy shook his head with a sharp jerk, taking Leo's meaning instantly. "I daresay I will quickly regain my sea legs, but no. It does not call to me." His lips thinned, and a shiver travelled up his spine. "In fact, the thought of our old life finding me strikes fear in my heart."

"Then why take on the assignment at all?" he goaded. "I know how ill at ease you were with your station—particularly in those last few years. You once said you would rather—"

"I know what I said," Percy interjected, cutting his friend a sideways glance. "And I stand by my statement." He huffed a breath, shaking his head. "And *ill at ease* is indeed too tame for what I felt then, for what I *still* feel. Down that path lies villainy, and I bloody refuse to become my father."

Leo lifted a brow. "So I shall ask again: why take on the assignment at all?"

"You know very well why. I'm skilled at combat, and I'm an experienced deck hand. They need me."

"Is that the *only* reason?"

Jaw clenched, Percy spun in another turn. But didn't answer.

Leo, the blighter, nodded his understanding as he stretched out his legs and crossed them at the ankle, waiting patiently for Percy to continue.

Hell, but this was not to be borne. Fear, guilt, and trepidation all warred within him, blustering and whirling about like the tempestuous sea.

"The woman I met last night..."

One of Leo's blond eyebrows lifted. "The tryst in the gazebo."

Percy nodded. "That was Miss Heather Morgan."

Leo spluttered and sat bolt upright. "The hell it was!"

"I spotted her—the woman with the black feathered costume and the ribbons in her hair—just before the unmasking. She was dancing with Hanley. Hell's tits, Leo, I thought she was a widow. But then I saw her, and when I came home, I saw the streaks of blood..." He cursed once more, recalling the horror and burning shame he'd felt at seeing the proof that he'd taken her maidenhead smeared on his cock. "She was so sure of herself, so damned seductive. And I...so sodding desperate."

"*Miss Morgan*. You had sex with Miss *Morgan*?" Leo scratched at his chin and raked his fingers through his blond hair. "Does she know it was you?"

Percy groaned. "I don't know. I daresay it's possible, but we agreed to keep our identities concealed and our masks on during the encounter. And she whispered throughout, as did I.

"But in mere hours our assignment together commences, Leo." His gut churned and his chest clenched.

"Have you a plan?"

Percy had thought about it in depth, and his options, while plentiful, were reduced to one when it came to both his and Miss Morgan's honour. After the way he'd been raised, he would never leave a woman to rear a child of his alone. *Please let her not be carrying my child*. Despite his desire to work, he had more than enough wealth to keep himself and a potential family comfortable for the remainder of their lives.

While he'd despised it at large, piracy had indeed provided an adequate fortune. He'd intended to bequeath it to Miss Lizzy Notley and any other children of Leo and Juliana, in addition to a tidy sum allocated to aiding orphaned children on the streets of London. That, now, would have to change.

Another groan rumbled through his chest, and he rubbed his eyes once more. Even should Miss Morgan *not* be pregnant, he would do the right thing.

"Yes, Leo. I have a plan."

THE CARRIAGE TRUNDLED over the cobblestones, jostling Heather against the squabs. Conflicting emotions waged battle in her heart: anticipation for the adventure and assignment before her, and sorrow at leaving her home, her friends… her plants.

Horses' hooves thundered along the road, and the carriage's wheels rumbled as they carried her to her future.

"Stop with those dreadful, unsightly tears," her aunt, Lady Budford, snapped. "You'll make Lord Hanley regret his decision if he sees you crying, your face a horrible mottled red. And we cannot have him leaving you behind."

Heather frowned. "I'm not crying, Aunt. I—"

"Don't be impertinent," she snapped, her grey eyes flashing with irritation. "Your marriage to the earl will provide us with an auspicious connection that will benefit your cousins. You cannot always be so selfish like your mother." She sighed happily, a small smile quirking her lips. "Oh, it shall be lovely to have you out of my home, Calluna."

A familiar twinge of pain sliced through Heather's heart. After her parents' death, she'd been left upon her aunt and uncle's doorstep, and while they'd provided her with the necessary items for survival, she'd never once felt welcomed or cared for. She'd never understood the animosity her aunt carried for her mother, but it was shown in every one of her actions toward Heather.

"All those ghastly plants stinking up the house," her aunt continued. "We've at last satisfied the obligation to my dreadful sister and that boring plant lover she married, and we can be free of you."

"I'm pleased you're happy, Aunt," Heather murmured.

Fury flared in Lady Budford's eyes. "You'd best be pleased, ungrateful girl! I might have tossed you to the streets once you'd reached eighteen, and then where would you be? That's *seven* extra years I've kept you housed and fed out of the goodness of my own heart—not that you needed any more food, for pity's sake. Just look at you," she sneered.

Heather bit back the retort that threatened to escape. It would do little good to make the woman angrier. Heather knew her aunt was wrong, and that was all that mattered.

At least *someone* found her desirable. Heat flared in her belly at the memory of the mystery man the previous night. He'd wanted to further their acquaintance, mayhap engage in another tryst... Her stomach swooped. She'd wanted it as well, but it simply couldn't work. It was proof, however, that men were capable of admiring her, regardless of her body's shape or size or the colour of her hair.

Early summer sun glinted off the surface of the Thames, and ships and smaller boats spotted the water. The earl's carriage rolled along the uneven road, their possessions having been loaded earlier that morning and their staff—including Cordelia—riding behind.

Their equipage rolled to a halt, rocking as the footmen dismounted from the rear. Shouts, lapping water, and the call of gulls rose up from beyond the carriage's walls, but Heather scarcely heard it for her pulse pounding in her head.

This is it, her heart whispered. Her adventure was about to begin.

The door swung outward, and a footman's helping hand reached in.

"Get out, idiot girl!" her aunt groused, shoving at Heather's arm.

Swallowing back her retort, Heather accepted the footman's hand and stepped down. The scent of decaying fish hit her instantly, and she discreetly breathed through her mouth. Men stomped to and fro around her, carrying boxes and barrels.

The sun heated her through her pale green petticoats, the gentle breeze providing little relief. Even through the clouds, and the undoubtedly rough waters between England and the Americas, the sun would be her constant companion through the summer, hovering somewhere above. The sun and her teammates, Percy and Cordelia.

At that moment, Percy ought to be somewhere on the frigate, working alongside the crew. Cordelia, acting as her maid and chaperone, was disembarking from her carriage even now.

Her moment had arrived.

PERSPIRATION DAMPENED Percy's skin and stained his uniform. The stale, hot air was nigh unbearable, and he was very much looking forward to the relief of some wind.

He deposited the barrel he carried into the hold and returned to the quarterdeck. Wiping his brow with the sleeve of his coat, he turned his attention to the docks.

Four carriages had arrived carrying the Earl of Hanley, Miss Heather Morgan, their servants, and Cordelia. Few of the earl's staff would join him and Heather on their frigate; most would journey upon the frigate that would follow. Hanley had apparently bemoaned the expense, but not only did his belongings take up far too much room in the hold, the safest way to travel the seas was in pairs. The second ship would be roughly a half day's journey behind them, should they encounter any severe inclement weather and require aid.

On the shore, the earl waved his hands about, first blustering at his valet, then turning to shout at Heather. Percy frowned, his gut clenching as he attempted to make sense of the man's angry gestures.

The earl pointed at Cordelia, then back at his own milling staff and the frigates. Heather retorted, pointing at her chest, then at Cordelia. Heather's aunt stepped in, gripping Heather's shoulders and gesturing plaintively at the earl. *Fuck.*

It would appear that he had decided to not permit Cordelia on board.

"Back t' work!" a man growled behind Percy.

Brow creasing in a scowl, Percy turned and retrieved another barrel. The necessities to sail had already been completed on both ships, with the exception of preparing the oars for their careful navigation through the mouth of the Thames, but the earl had strongly demanded that his particular items be added to their hold throughout the journey. Percy would be amazed if the earl had not demanded the captain's quarters as well.

Unable to help himself, his gaze darted back toward the docks, and he caught one last glimpse of Heather before he went belowdecks. Bubbles of nervous energy rippled through his abdomen. They'd been *intimate* last night... His heart gave a hard thump at the memory of their tryst.

Focus, Percy, he chided himself.

If Cordelia was unable to continue with her role, Percy would be required to provide additional support. Hanley was a dangerous man, and now was decidedly not the time for Percy to lose sight of their task—and the role he had to play.

Muffled shouting and thumping footfalls filled Heather's ears as she followed a large man across the upper deck. Fury and frustration stiffened her spine. She must speak with Percy. The earl—her affianced—refused admittance to Cordelia, who'd been meant to act as her lady's maid. Now, she was down her closest confidante in this assignment. The woman was meant to infiltrate the earl's staff to glean information, but now the entirety of it was up to Heather.

She stifled another sigh of agitation and attempted to

focus on the man ahead of her. *Setbacks are to be expected*, she reminded herself. *I can do this.*

The ship—the *Sapphire*—was rather larger than she had expected, with three masts, streams of organized ropes, and cannons spaced evenly along either side of the ship. The helm and three small structures were situated near the rear of the ship. Men strode with purpose about the deck, and young men clung to the masts and sails like children climbing trees.

It was entirely new, this world on a frigate. Undoubtedly, the other decks would prove just as curious.

"M' name's Stubbs," her guide said over one broad shoulder. "This deck is called th' quarterdeck." He gestured around them with one arm.

Heather nodded.

He led her to a narrow stairwell that rather seemed more of a ladder, and descended to the second deck.

"These steps r' called th' companionway," he noted. "As y' can see, this deck's th' gun deck." He pointed toward the rear of the ship. "Them doors lead t' th' cap'n's cabin."

Heather glanced around the deck. Sunlight shone through the gaping holes in the deck above. Lord knew what they were for, but it certainly brightened the space. Cannons lined both sides of the deck. Next to each was a bucket and a stack of cannonballs. Toward the front was what appeared to be several cook tops and ovens with a chimney stack that rose up through the deck above.

The man named Stubbs led her down another ladder—companionway—onto the third deck. A chill of unease raced up her spine. Hanging lanterns lit the space, swinging slowly with the gentle sway of the ship. *Fire.* Her pulse skipped, and she swallowed back the groan that threatened. Instead, she forced her attention back to the remainder of the space.

The centre and front of the deck were lined with tables, benches, and buckets, and had multiple sacks that hung from beams above the tables. The rear part of the deck was lined with what appeared to be cabinetry, though they were separated by a wall that divided the last portion of the deck.

"This is th' mess deck," Stubbs said. "Th' men sleep in 'ammocks above th' tables, an' there"—he gestured toward the cabinets—"are th' officers' cabins. Yours is this'n on th' end."

Heather nodded her understanding.

"There're three cabins in each row, before th' dividing wall," the sailor continued. "On th' other side is th' wardroom and four additional officers' cabins on each wall. Each cabin along th' wall gets larger t'ward th' bow, yers being th' smallest, th' earl claiming th' largest."

Heather nodded once more. "Thank you, Stubbs."

"Aye," he grunted. "Th' surgeon's in th' orlop if y' 'ave need of 'im."

With that, the man tugged on his forelock and ascended the companionway, leaving her alone at the entrance of her cabin. Men rushed around the deck and stomped overhead, no doubt preparing for their departure.

Her stomach twisting painfully, she opened the door and stepped inside.

She squeezed her eyes shut for a moment, waiting until she had acclimatized before taking in the space only just wide enough to accommodate the hanging bed at the back wall. On Heather's left was a short, narrow chest of two drawers, atop of which sat two of her plants: *Marrubium vulgare* and *Hypericum perforatum*, the yellow and white blooms on the herbs looking sad in the dim room.

Across from the chest was what appeared to be a fabric seat with foldable wooden legs on the sides, and on the floor beneath the hanging bed was a chamber pot and one of her trunks.

It was a sad space, indeed, scarcely large enough for the few items already inside. Where were her other plants? Where *could* she keep them? They wouldn't survive without sunlight.

A soul-deep sigh overtook her. This would be her home for the coming weeks—or months. She'd best find a way to not only keep her plants alive, but also make this small cabin feel like home.

Tap-tap. A knock sounded at her door, and she turned to answer it.

Standing just outside was a young woman whose blue eyes veritably glittered with excitement, her mobcap vibrating with each of her heaving breaths.

The maid's thin lips curved upward as she curtseyed. "I've come to unpack your trunk, miss."

"Oh, of course. Thank you..."

"Berta, miss. I'm not ordinarily a lady's maid, I'm afraid, but I'll do my best to serve you. I usually work in the kitchens, you see. My main duties are to help the cook and do washing. But I can help you, too, when you need it."

"Berta." Heather returned the maid's smile. "A pleasure, I'm sure. I shall leave you to it."

The maid stepped away from the doorway while Heather slid past. She might have stayed to chat with the woman, but there was scarcely enough space for one of them within the small room, let alone two.

Unsure what to do with herself and not wanting to get in the way of the sailors, she ascended to the bright quarterdeck and settled herself near the railing. Men climbed the masts, wrapping themselves around the sail posts and adjusting the ropes, while others stood at the bottom of the masts and pulled ropes from there. There were sailors with buckets and barrels, and yet more walking with purpose or shouting orders. Two men stood at the helm, engaged in deep discussion.

Heather wondered what position Percy had taken upon

the frigate. Would he be belowdecks, mayhap working the guns, or was he among these men, climbing, tying, or carrying heavy things?

Her skin warmed quickly beneath her frock, the sky clear and brilliant and the air heavy with humidity. She could scarcely breathe for the heat! Perspiration beaded along her hairline and between her breasts, and she fought the urge to scratch at it.

The broad back of a tall man caught her eye and kindled a spark of recognition, but it disappeared below deck before she could ascertain if it belonged to Percy.

Her thoughts drifted back to the mystery man of the night before, and her stomach gave a happy wobble. That man had been glorious indeed. He would be in her thoughts for many years to come.

Someone hollered from the gun deck, and then there was the shuffling of feet and the scraping of wood on wood.

Heather turned, bracing herself against the balustrade, and peered over the edge of the ship. From the deck below came long wooden oars through small doors along the boat's side.

"Cat the anchor!" a man shouted.

Three men rushed over to the front of the ship and quickly pulled on some ropes.

The oars splashed into the water of the Thames, and a rhythmic shouting began beneath her feet.

"*Row, row, row!*"

Gradually, the *Sapphire* drifted away from the crowded Pool of London and manoeuvred between the other moored ships until they were no longer surrounded by land. Merchant ships sailed past in both directions, and Heather wondered if she could reach one of them if she leapt from the *Sapphire* and swam. It was ludicrous, of course, and she had a duty to complete, but the curiosity was there...

Despite her eagerness for the assignment, her chest gave a

squeeze of melancholy as she watched England gradually grow smaller. She would dearly miss her friends, her plants, and the comfort of the Bow Street offices.

With another scrape of wood against wood, the oars disappeared into the *Sapphire*'s belly, and the small doors closed. Hurried footsteps sounded from below before men scrambled to their stations on the quarterdeck.

Heather bent over the rail, desirous to minimize the space she consumed on the deck and to watch the spray of water against the hull.

"Miss Morgan?" a tentative voice said behind her.

Startled out of her thoughts, Heather spun around.

Her pulse fluttered, and a smile stole over her lips. "Percy!"

CHAPTER 5

*P*ulse fluttering madly in his chest, Percy stepped tentatively closer. *Christ*, but seeing Heather so soon after... It was as though he was seeing her with new eyes. Her hair glowed copper in the sunlight, her eyes glittered green, and her cheeks were flushed from the sun. She was a vision. He now knew what her full lips felt like beneath his, how soft her skin was to his touch, and how damned *good* she tasted... His body hummed at her nearness.

"It's good to see you," she said breathily, taking in his bared feet and calves, his slops, his ill-fitting blue coat, and his loosened cravat.

He knew how he appeared. Not only could he not don his customary ocean-faring attire, but he was now a man in service to the Crown and would wear what his superiors deemed fit. He mustn't cause a disturbance. If he drew undue attention and they discovered the truth of who he was, they would likely have him keelhauled.

He cleared his throat. "I observed your disagreement on the docks. Was Cordelia unable to come aboard, or is she to sail upon the frigate that follows?"

Heather's gaze turned stormy, and she gave a sideways glance to ensure they were unheard. "The earl barred her admittance on board entirely. It is just us two continuing the assignment."

Pulse tripping again, he nodded once. "We must work quickly to find what you require."

"Tonight?"

A shout came from behind him, and Percy straightened. "*Aye!*" He smiled apologetically at Heather. "I must go, but I'm off duty at dusk. Would you, perhaps, wish to play a game of cards?" He lifted an eyebrow in suggestion.

"I would be delighted," she returned with a quirk of her lips.

With a tug of his forelock, he turned and found his post at the base of the mizzen-mast, gathering the ropes in his hand. He turned his gaze upward toward the topmen who worked aloft, matching his movements to theirs. The motions came naturally to Percy, having done the job for years before captaining his own ship. Before then, he'd shared the role of topman, and then captain of the top, before he grew too large for the job.

Navigating the masts, rigging, and the watch from aloft required intelligence, agility, and strength. One mislaid line in the middle of a chase, high winds, or a battle could result in the loss of the entire crew.

On the *Sapphire*, Percy worked on deck, handling the lines and controlling the sails. It wasn't an ideal job while he was attempting to aid Heather in uncovering the earl's treachery, but he could certainly help while off duty.

His gaze drifted back toward her, where she stood at the rail and watched her homeland become but a blemish on the horizon. *Christ*, but he ought to have confessed that *he* was the man she'd—

But he hadn't the faintest notion of how to tell her. He'd

thought about it for most of the morning while completing menial tasks, but he couldn't devise a single method of telling her that wouldn't see him slapped or spurned. The woman deserved to know, blast it. He detested the thought, however, that she might believe he'd deliberately sought her out to relieve her of her maidenhead.

Indeed, she had to know—particularly if their encounter resulted in her getting with child. A shiver raced down his spine. The thought of becoming a father was terrifying, but he would stand by his morals. Whether or not she was pregnant, Heather would have him by her side.

THE ORANGE GLOW of the sun gently faded into dusk, forcing Heather to squint at the pages of her book. She'd been able to bring only a select few volumes on the journey, and this was one of her favourite books on horticulture. Leaning closer to the page, she ignored the ache in her back and the numbness of her bottom as she sat upon the hard planks of the quarterdeck.

A shadow approached, blocking her view of the book and looming over her.

"The evening meal's been served, miss," Berta said softly. "The earl requests your presence in the wardroom."

Heather's lips firmed into a grim line. "Thank you, Berta."

The maid dipped in a curtsey and departed, hurrying down the companionway leading to the gun deck.

Heather sighed, wisps of her hair catching in the warm wind and tickling her cheeks. The wind had, indeed, been a relief from the heat of the sun, though she imagined that it would be no protection against her tendency to freckle.

Despite her optimistic intentions, she hadn't the opportunity to search her fiancé's belongings that afternoon. The man had kept close to his quarters, apparently barking orders at his valet and footmen.

With a subtle stretch, Heather rose to her feet. The frigate rocked, and she caught her footing, tucked her book beneath one arm, and descended both companionways leading to the mess deck. The scent of citrus and beef hit her first, and her mouth watered. Then she smelled the freshly baked rolls, and her stomach rumbled with interest.

Hastening her steps, she tossed the book on her hanging bed and made her way into the wardroom. There, a long dining table covered with gleaming plates, silverware, and two candelabras was surrounded by men in blue, cream, and gold naval uniforms. That was, of course, with the exception of the Earl of Shite, who still wore his green suit of clothes with a cream waistcoat and silver trim.

"You're late," the earl announced, his yellowed teeth showing behind a curled lip.

"My apologies," she mumbled, curtseying.

She eyed the candelabras dubiously, then sat in the remaining vacant seat at the earl's side. He huffed his disapproval, giving her a sideways glare. *Just you wait, oh Earl of Shite*, her inner voice whispered. *I shall be victorious in the end.* She smiled tentatively at the men around the table and picked up a roll.

The other men nodded politely in turn before breaking into small discussions among themselves. The low hum of voices and the gentle clink of cutlery filled the room.

"You don't need that," the earl muttered sideways lifting his brow at her roll.

"I'm hungry," she murmured back.

His gaze narrowed on her. "You're mine now, Calluna, and you shall do precisely what I say. You are permitted one piece of meat and a glass of Madeira."

Indignation flared in her chest. "You'll have me starve, sir?"

"Indeed not," he replied with a jovial smile that failed to reach his cold eyes. "You'll have a piece of meat."

"You must at least permit me some citrus, sir. It's imperative to stave off scurvy."

He sighed gustily. "*One* piece, no more."

Well, this certainly won't do. Her aunt and uncle had attempted precisely the same. Heather hadn't accepted their attempt at control and manipulation then, and she wouldn't accept it from the earl now.

With light fingers, she palmed her roll and hid it within the folds of her skirts.

"I saw you speaking rather intimately with a crewmate earlier," the earl growled in her ear a moment later. "You seemed quite familiar with the man. Who is he?"

Gooseflesh spread over Heather's scalp and down her back, and she suppressed the shiver that threatened. The earl was far too observant—that boded ill for her assignment.

"I don't know his name," she lied dismissively. "I asked him where I might stand to better view our departure while also ensuring that I did not disturb the crew's productivity."

His blue eyes glinted, and his hand slid beneath the table to palm her thigh. Heather stiffened at the contact, alarm spreading in her chest. He squeezed. Hard. For a heartbeat, she sat in immobile shock at the man's bold aggression, fury riding her. Percy had taught her at least twelve ways in which to incapacitate this bastard, but she was meant to be intimidated by his power and fearful of the punishment he might bring down on her, her family, and her friends.

She gave a faint wince—for the man would expect her not only to show her pain, but to be cowed by his show of dominance.

"I'll not be made a cuckold, Calluna," he whispered

through gritted teeth. "Neither here aboard the ship, nor during our life in the Americas."

"O-of course, your lordship." *Beautiful performance, Heather.*

A genuine smile pulled at his lips, and his gaze shone with satisfaction as he sat back and bit into a roll.

Bastard.

She cut into a piece of meat and forked it into her mouth, taking no notice of its flavour or the texture, her mind entirely occupied with how she might carry out her search for the earl's secretive documents.

HEAVY FOOTFALLS REVERBERATED OVERHEAD as Heather waited silently in her gloomy cabin. Faint light shone in through the upper portion of her door, which was comprised merely of narrow wood slats—decidedly inappropriate, for it afforded her almost no privacy.

She listened carefully for the earl's loud, inebriated blustering as he ascended to the quarterdeck. This was her opportunity.

Anticipation driving her, she padded the two steps to her door and inched it open, peering through to see if the way was clear of the earl's men. Several sailors were eating a late meal in the "mess," while numerous others had retreated to their hammocks. No one paid her any mind.

A jolt of nerves raced through her middle. Percy had said that he would be on either the gun deck or the quarterdeck making casual conversation with one or more of the earl's staff. This was most decidedly her time.

With quick strides, Heather slipped from her cabin and into the empty wardroom. The earl's cabin was said to be at the far end of her row. She peered between the wood slats to be certain before sneaking inside. The room was dimly lit—precisely as hers had been—but the light coming in between the slats on the door provided just enough for her purpose. The space was bigger, both in width and length, but it was largely the same as hers.

Move quickly.

Her pulse sped, and her lips quirked with a grin as she commenced her search. She began with the chest of drawers on her left. Atop it was a glass of water, a comb, mirror, and unlit candle, which she ignored, going instead directly for the top drawer.

The earl's valet had done a fine job organizing the earl's things. Fine enough that it was directly evident that nothing was hidden in the drawer. Nor the next. Nor the last. In an attempt at thoroughness, she inspected the bottom and underside of each drawer, in the event that there was a false bottom where one might hide documents.

Nothing. *Blast.*

The chest of drawers was bolted both to the floor and the wall—no doubt to keep the occupant safe in inclement weather—so there was no way in which someone might hide something there.

A thump from overhead made her pulse skip, and she stilled to listen for any sign of the earl's return. There was no pugnacious shouting forthcoming, so she lowered to her knees and bent to inspect beneath the bed.

It was darker there, but she could discern the outlines of a chamber pot and two pairs of shoes. No lockbox or hidden paperwork. Careful to not disturb the turned-down bedclothes, Heather reached her arms beneath the curved mattress, stretching and feeling for any indication of something hidden. *Nothing. Again.*

Frustration and desperation flooded her. Where would the Earl of Shite keep damning documents? She'd *thought* he might keep them close... She stood to examine the coats, waist-coats, and shirts hanging on the right side of the small space. There were a few pound notes, but naught else.

A steady tread entered the wardroom, and Heather froze. *Is it the earl's valet?* Her pulse drummed against her ribs, and she silently cursed the rush in her ears.

Tap-tap. "*Heather?*" Percy whispered.

Her breath left her in a *whoosh*, and she reached for the door. She pushed it open to reveal Percy, his hair tousled and cheeks flushed from the wind. *Blimey.* Her stomach gave an entirely different sort of wobble, and warmth flooded her abdomen decidedly against her wishes.

"Percy," she returned breathlessly. "How did you fare?"

His gaze scanned her features as he shook his head. "Nothing. You?"

She scrunched her nose and stepped into the wardroom, closing the door behind herself. "Not a single thing, blast it."

They strode together through the room and back toward the mess. Despite the impropriety, the urge to touch him—even in passing—was too much to be borne. *Focus.*

"Surely the man didn't leave such documentation behind," she whispered incredulously.

Percy shook his head once more. "If he did, then he's no intention of returning to England. I daresay we're just looking in the wrong place."

"More reconnaissance?" she asked.

"More reconnaissance."

CHAPTER 6

"*I*'ll not warn you again, Calluna," the Earl of Shite said, hot in Heather's ear. "*No toast*. You may have one piece of citrus and one egg."

Hell, but if she didn't find those documents quickly, she would undoubtedly perish of starvation.

With a satisfied smile, the earl returned to the discussion between the officers at the table. It was obvious to none but Heather that his *true* attention was fixed on *her*. She took a sip of the weak tea in her cup, the lukewarm liquid churning in her stomach.

The need to retort, to snap at the man who so clearly enjoyed exerting his dominance—or what he *perceived* to be his dominance—was high. But for the purpose of this assignment, she would play this part, and play it well.

The blackguard shifted at her side, his gaze still on the officer across from them, while his hand slid beneath the table to once more rest on her thigh. The bruises he'd caused the night before throbbed, and she pasted on a smile and cut into a piece of egg.

"I hear tell there are clouds in the distance," an officer said. "Mayhap this evening we shall see rain."

Heather traced a finger along the table's upper ridge, the wooden perimeter no doubt meant to keep the items on the table from sliding off. And she listened. The discussion turned from the weather to their stores of food, then to the theatre and riding—nothing that would give Heather any insight into the earl's activities, or proof thereof.

She finished her slice of orange and single boiled egg, then drank the last of her cold tea. Her stomach rumbled.

The earl's hand tightened on her thigh, squeezing hard, as though the pain he caused would somehow eliminate her hunger. *Bastard.*

While it had never bothered her before, Heather acknowledged that she was a larger woman. She doubted her weight was the only reason the earl exerted this control, however. It was likely that he would have done the same to his previous affianced had Heather and her team not intervened and freed the smaller woman from the earl's clutches. No matter what the blackguard did in an effort to dominate her, though, she was grateful that it was *her*, and not another woman, to suffer.

"Just bloody *find* it!" The earl's growl broke her from her momentary reverie.

"I've tried, your lordship, but there are numerous trunks," the earl's valet said plaintively. "I took the liberty of preparing the blue waistcoat for the morrow, in the event that you might—"

"Not the blue, blast it," Hanley hissed. "Just find the grey one."

A bead of sweat rolled down the valet's temple. "Of course, your lordship. I shall look again."

"See that you do." The earl turned back to the officers observing the exchange and scoffed. "Really, how hard is it to find a waistcoat?"

Heather ignored the murmured responses from the officers as her pulse skipped and her thoughts whirled. *The hold.* Of course! How foolish of her to not consider it before now. The earl had packed crates, casks, and trunks full of his nonsense—far too much for just one frigate to hold. That was precisely where she must look.

NEARLY EVERY ONE of Percy's muscles burned. It had been years since he had manned the lines on a ship, and his body was making its feelings known. He swallowed the last of his watery grog and leaned his elbows on the table.

The sailors around him broke their fast, talked, and joked with one another, some eyeing the earl's two maids as they ate. And Percy waited. He wanted another opportunity to talk to Heather, to sort out his feelings about the woman he'd come to know in London and the woman whose body he'd learned so intimately...

It was as though he'd never truly *seen* her before that night. He'd known her, of course, and had *felt* things, but she'd been his student and entirely off-limits. Now he was beguiled and wanted to learn more about her.

The door to the wardroom swung open, and Percy's breath froze as Heather's gaze caught his. She lifted a brow and notched her chin upward before ascending to the gun deck. *She has information.*

Percy hastily cleared the table and followed Heather up to the bustling quarterdeck. Men darted about, most beginning their shift, while some withdrew for their turn to sleep.

He spotted Heather at the taffrail. Her chignon was windswept, just as wild and unpredictable as the woman herself.

With a grin—and decidedly more nervous fluttering in his

gut—Percy strode over to rest his forearms next to hers, gazing out at the seemingly infinite ocean. The early morning sun heated him through his uniform, the warmth gratefully broken by the steady, cooling wind. The ocean splashed as they glided through the water, and for a moment the salt air consumed him.

"Good morning," he murmured.

"Mmm," she hummed. "Is it?"

She cast him a sideways glance, one brow lifted, and her lips quirked in a fucking delicious grin.

She huffed a laugh. "The *hold*, Percy. I don't know why I hadn't considered it before, but it makes perfect sense that the earl would store any damning evidence there. No doubt he assumes that no one would willingly suffer the inconvenience of searching through a plethora of excess to happen upon his dastardly dealings."

Percy returned her grin. "He is wrong on that score."

"Indeed, he is. Are you up for the challenge?"

His pulse quickened. "Always. Shall we?"

He moved to push away from the taffrail, but Heather stopped him with a touch. Sparks of desire raced up his arm, through his centre, and straight to his cock. *Sweet fuck.* He bit back a groan. The woman had the ability to render him hard at a simple touch.

Damn. He *really* ought to tell her about their tryst. But how?

Heather cleared her throat and dropped her hand to her side, fisting it in the material of her pretty green frock. "The earl's valet is down there"—she swallowed and cleared her throat once more—"searching for one of the earl's waistcoats. We must wait until he resurfaces."

His gaze held hers as her cheeks flushed with a warmth that he longed to touch. "Then we wait."

"THIS IS ONE OF HIS," Percy grunted, sliding a chest toward Heather.

The gentle glow of candlelight flickered over his striking profile, and Heather's gut swooped. Whether it was from her fear of the fire or these inopportune feelings for Percy, she didn't know. Regardless of the reason, it ought to stop. Oughtn't it?

Her initial uneasiness aside, they'd slipped into the hold without drawing a single glance askance. The earl had shouted himself hoarse and promptly taken a nap, while his staff took some much-needed respite and the seamen went about their duties. No one looked, no one cared—not while the earl was asleep.

She huffed a breath and stretched her arms above her head in an effort to dispel the tightness in her shoulders. They'd been searching through the Earl of Shite's effects for nearly three quarters of an hour and had found naught but some entirely repulsive literature.

She would grant that it would not seem so repugnant—in fact, she might have enjoyed it for some light reading—if not for the awareness that it was the *earl's*. Another shiver of revulsion raced down her spine.

Percy laughed, the low, husky sound echoing in the close confines of the frigate's hold. "You *must* stop thinking about it, Heather. You'll give yourself the headache."

She frowned at him, despite the buzz of awareness humming through her middle. "I'm trying, blast it!"

He laughed again and opened another crate to inspect its contents. Heather did the same, lifting a lid and gazing inside. It was full of hessians, brushes, and cloths. She rolled her eyes.

"How many boots could a man need on a voyage to the

Americas in the summer?" she murmured, tracing her fingers along the seams of the trunk's inner lining.

There was a loose thread, and she picked at it.

"If his valet takes care of them properly, I daresay he wouldn't need more than two," Percy returned, setting the crate aside and selecting another.

"There are at least five pairs in here." She tugged at the loose thread, and the seam came apart, leaving a gaping hole along the trunk's side. *"Bugger it.* His valet's going to know someone interfered with this one; I've gone and—"

She paused, staring at the opening.

Percy snorted, but turned to look at her when she went silent. "What is it?"

"I think this seam was *meant* to open. This looks like it was a false stitch."

Pulse fluttering with hope and exhilaration, Heather slid her hand into the narrow hole. Her fingers probed, stretching out in search of...anything.

Her breath caught in her throat. Something crinkled beneath her touch. *There!*

Using the tips of her index and middle fingers, she pinched the pieces of parchment and pulled. A squeak of delight escaped her as she held them out.

"What do they say?" Percy asked.

Heather placed the folded pieces of parchment on her lap and opened one.

She gave the document a quick scan, and dread washed over her.

"Holy hell," she breathed.

Her skin grew cold, her limbs trembling.

"Jesus, what is it, Heather?" Percy asked, concern lining his features.

"This says that despite the Royal Marriages Act of 1772, the Prince Regent's marriage to Maria Fitzherbert was legitimate—that they *did*, in fact, garner consent from the reigning monarch, and that it was declared in council."

Percy cursed under his breath.

Her heart in her throat, Heather set the parchment aside and picked up another. Then gasped. "This is the certificate of birth of a *son*, born to Maria Fitzherbert on—"

"It's a forgery," Percy interjected. "It has to be."

Heather's gaze darted to his. At some point, he'd retrieved the parchment she'd just set aside and examined it.

"Are you certain?" she asked.

He notched his chin toward her lap. "Read the next."

And she did.

"This is a letter from '*G*' to '*H*'—who I shall presume is Hanley." She gasped, then choked and gave a spluttered cough.

"Hell, Heather, are you all right?" Percy leaned forward to put a hand to her shoulder, and another jolt of heat raced through her.

"Fine," she wheezed, handing the parchment to him.

He tilted the parchment toward the candlelight, and his eyes fairly bulged as he read. "Sodding hell, Heather!" he hissed. "This contains plans to overthrow the Crown. It asks if the recipient has properly hidden the forgeries"—he waves the other documents in his free hand—"mentions this author's intent to support '*H*' in parliament upon his return to England, and explains what they've done to provide passage upon a Royal Navy frigate. It then explicitly demands that '*H*' destroy this letter upon reading."

"*Sodding hell*, indeed," Heather breathed, fisting her frigid, trembling hands against her chest. Her pulse raced, and an overwhelming swell of conflicting emotions rushed through her, namely triumph...and a healthy amount of panic.

Percy's wide gaze met hers through the flickering candle-light, his chest rising and falling with his rapid breaths. "This document implicates these two people for high treason."

"He must have kept the letter—instead of destroying it, as demanded—in order to extort something from 'G.'"

Percy nodded in thought. "You don't imagine 'G' is the Prince Regent, do you?"

"He was in love with Maria Fitzherbert. Mayhap this is a way to dissolve his marriage to Princess Caroline?" Heather offered.

"I don't see the logic in fabricating a son," Percy murmured, glancing up toward the orlop above them. "But we haven't the time to ruminate on it at the moment."

"Noted."

With sure movements, Heather refolded the proof she needed to put Hanley on trial, stuffed it—*carefully*—between her breasts, and helped Percy rearrange the crates and chests back to the way they'd found them.

SQUINTING into the setting afternoon sun, Heather strode across the quarterdeck with another book on horticulture under one arm. She caught Percy's gaze as he handled some ropes, and walked casually toward him.

"Are they safe?" he asked in a hushed tone, his gaze fixed on the lines above.

"Mm-hmm," she hummed in the affirmative. She'd hidden them amongst the pages of her mother's journal.

He gave a subtle nod, and she continued past him to rest her elbows on the ship's railing. She turned her face into the wind, relishing the cool air on her flushed cheeks.

She'd done it. She'd found damning evidence against the earl. All that was required of her now was to discreetly present the information to the *Sapphire*'s captain, Sir Willard, have him put the earl in the brig, and turn both frigates around to return to England.

Her gaze slid toward the helm, where the Earl of Shite stood barking orders at the captain and his first mate. She sighed, despite the wild fluttering of her pulse.

The only obstacle was to find a time in which she could speak to the captain without the earl or his staff around to intervene.

"Pardon me, Miss Morgan," a hesitant voice said from beside her.

Heather turned to see one of the earl's footmen standing close by, and she offered him a tentative smile. "Yes?"

"His lordship has requested your presence in the mess."

Her stomach gave a dip. The earl could not possibly know that she'd pilfered his documents...could he? Her gaze flicked over the footman's shoulder to where the earl had been. But he was gone.

"Very well," she capitulated.

The young man stepped aside to let her lead the way to the companionway. He followed close behind her as she descended to the mess deck, and all the while Heather's nerves grew increasingly fraught.

The moment both her feet touched the deck's wooden planks, a hand clamped tightly around her upper arm. *Clunk.* Her book dropped as she spun to face the earl.

"I warned you," he growled.

"Warned me?" she asked.

"You must learn acquiescence and obedience, and I intend to—"

"Are they not one and the same?" she asked smartly.

His grip tightened, his fingertips digging painfully into the soft flesh of her upper arm as he dragged her toward her cabin. Two of his footmen stood close by, observing the exchange, while the naval sailors milling about the mess deck watched from afar.

She would be able to defend herself against the earl and at

least one of his men, but if others stepped in to defend the blackguard, she would most certainly lose.

"I'll not tolerate a rebellious nature," the earl snarled. "And I'll *not* be made a cuckold."

They reached her cabin, and he spun her around to slam her back against the opened door's frame. Sparks danced behind her eyelids as her head knocked hard against the wood. She groaned and attempted to put a hand to her head, but the earl pinned her arms at her sides and pressed his body into hers.

Revulsion roiled in her gut, and she gritted her teeth against it.

"In the coming weeks you shall come to realize, Calluna," he breathed against her cheek, "just how dangerous a man I can be."

He pulled back to pinch her face in one of his hands, and she gasped at the sudden shock of pain. For an older man, he was a sight stronger than one might expect—more than *she* had expected, certainly.

One of the nearby footmen shuffled his feet, the sound barely audible over the busy activity of sailors stomping about the ship. With a huff of derision, the earl pulled back.

"Miss Morgan is not to leave her cabin," he said, his cold gaze still locked on hers.

Then, without warning, he grabbed her bodily and shoved her into her cabin. Heart in her throat, Heather stumbled forward and braced for inevitable impact. Despite her efforts, her hip struck the edge of the chest of drawers before she landed sideways upon her hanging bed. The pain, however, was naught when compared to the fear that ignited in her chest.

The earl meant to keep her locked in her cabin for the entirety of their month-long journey. *We cannot arrive in the Americas.* Dread crept up her spine in an alarming tingle. If she couldn't find a way to apprehend the earl before they reached land, her power would be significantly diminished, for surely the man's servants would fight on his behalf, and authorities in the Americas would do naught about a man accused of crimes across the ocean.

"Might I at least have my book?" she called out.

She ought to have requested a meeting with the captain directly upon discovering information on the earl, rather than ruminating on it. Hell, but she hadn't the faintest understanding of a captain's relationship to his crew; might he listen to a man such as Percy, particularly when it came to incriminatory information regarding an honoured guest? The earl might very well strike before Percy had the opportunity to speak with the captain, resulting in Percy being put in the brig instead.

Her breath all but froze in her chest. What had she done?

CHAPTER 7

A fortnight later

Clunk…*thunk…*clunk…*thunk—*clonk!

With a hard thump, Heather was tossed to the floor of her small cabin. Pain lanced through her head as it connected with the edge of her chest of drawers, and she pressed a hand to the spot, just above the hairline near her temple. She hissed, her head swimming and nausea churning in her belly.

Hot, sticky liquid oozed between her fingers, and she blinked numbly into obscurity, her stomach in upheaval.

Blinking, she attempted to dispel the foggy puzzlement clouding her mind. It had to be the middle of the night, for nary a sliver of light came from beyond her door. The air was heavy with salty humidity, and Heather groaned at the damp-ness between and under her breasts.

Clunk…thunk. The hanging bed rocked between the wall and the chest of drawers as the ship tilted. With a squeak,

Heather pressed her free hand to the wall and extended her legs so that she might avoid rolling into the door.

Her pulse sped, and her stomach heaved as the ship rocked in the opposite direction. She blinked again, struggling to comprehend the sudden movements in the pitch darkness.

A storm.

While her cabin hadn't any windows, it was impossible to know not only the hour, but also the weather. A storm, however, was decidedly obvious.

Clunk...thunk.

For the past fortnight, she'd been imprisoned in her cabin with a guard stationed at her door. Berta came by thrice daily to offer a pitiable meal, refill her pitcher, and empty both her chamberpot and washbasin, but said nary a word. At least Heather had been able to sodding *clean* herself.

Early in her imprisonment, she'd pleaded with her guard to send word to the captain, but the men were staffed by the earl and wouldn't risk punishment.

Clunk...thunk.

A warm, tickling sensation crept down her cheek and jaw, and she groaned.

"Bugger it all," she cursed, pressing her palm firmly to her temple.

The *Sapphire* pitched sideways, and her stomach lurched once more.

Hell. She must stand and dress if she was to slip past her guard and see the ship's surgeon.

ROPES CREAKED and voices sounded above as Percy attempted to sleep in his hammock. The steep waves of the storm rocked him in time with the other men around him, their hammocks occasionally bumping into each other.

Christ, but it had been an age since he'd slept aboard a ship. And while he truly hated to admit it to himself, he'd bloody well missed the satisfyingly deep sleep that he achieved while being rocked by the ocean. The sailor beside him, however, was a man to whom Percy had to grow accustomed, for the volume of his snoring alone was enough to wake the dead. It wasn't just the volume that bothered Percy but the *way* in which the man snored, wheezing, hissing, gurgling, and making all manner of other strange noises. In time, he knew, the sleep would come—as it had every night for the past fortnight—but until then, he would remain half-awake, listening to the cacophony of aggressive snoring from his neighbour.

Muffled rhythmic thumping came from the officers' cabins as their beds knocked against their cabin walls—though Christ knew he'd heard countless men fucking the boredom away behind those walls over the years—and Percy attempted to focus on the sound. Something else, however, captured his attention: grumbled cursing.

Percy's eyes snapped open. *There.* Another curse and a soft thump. It sounded very like Heather.

Despite himself, his pulse skipped.

A sodding fortnight had passed since they'd spoken, but he'd been so badly reprimanded for continuously attempting to speak with the captain that he'd lost not only his credibility but also his sway. No matter how he made the attempt, Heather's bloody guards refused to permit him a moment to speak with her, or to return her book.

Meanwhile Hanley, the shit sack, swaggered about the frigate, boldly demanding servitude and compliance from the crew.

Clunk.

Shifting in his hammock, Percy peered through the obscurity toward the officers' cabins. Heather's guard appeared to have left, either to join the day shift in sleep or to aid the men abovedecks during the storm.

Snick. A door latch opened, and a softly uttered "shite" floated toward him.

He huffed a quiet laugh. What was she doing?

With swift movements, he leapt out of his hammock and padded toward her on bared feet.

There was a soft click as Heather closed her door. The ship heaved once more, and she gripped the door's handle.

"*Ballocks,*" she muttered with feeling.

He grinned. "What are you doing?"

In a sudden rush of movement, she connected her fist to Percy's jaw, and pain flared hot as he cursed and groaned.

"Jesus, Heather, your training has done you well," Percy said, his voice muffled.

Heather snorted. "You startled me!"

"Clearly," he returned with a smirk. "I came to see if you required aid."

The ship pitched sideways, slamming her against her cabin's door.

"Damnation, are you okay?" he asked, stepping closer.

"Yes—*no.* Drat. How are you able to keep upright?"

"I keep a wider stance, and I'm accustomed to the *Sapphire*'s movement."

"Mmm," she hummed, then leaned closer to whisper, "I take it you were unable to speak privately with the captain?"

Guilt twisted in his chest. "He refused an audience with me—on numerous occasions."

Heather nodded. "I daresay it shall be a challenge to secure his support under these circumstances, but we must at least try."

She staggered sideways with a curse as the frigate rocked in a deep swell. Percy darted a hand out to steady her, and a zip of heat raced up his arm.

He cleared his throat. "While I'm pleased to see you, Heather, I must ask. Why are you about?"

She sighed. "I must see the surgeon, I'm afraid."

Thunder cracked overhead.

"The surgeon?" Percy asked, his voice tight.

"Yes. Might you show me the way?"

"Come."

He clasped her hand and wrapped it about his arm, pressing her firmly against his side as the *Sapphire* tilted once more. Percy leaned in the opposite direction as the swell, holding her up with him as he walked. His pulse raced at her touch, and he thought once more about telling her the truth about the masque. But so much time had elapsed that he worried she would be downright furious.

"Are you well, Heather?" Percy asked again.

"Well enough, I suppose." She paused, tightening her grip on his arm as the ship tilted. "Actually," she amended, "I'm not well, Percy. I feel so—"

Boom! Thunder cracked overhead.

They reached the companionway, and Percy released Heather to let her descend first. Faint light emanated from the one opened door at the end of the short corridor, and for a moment, Heather hesitated.

What had she been about to say?

Worry gnawed at Percy's stomach. She'd evidently been injured in some way.

The frigate pitched perilously sideways, and he clapped a hand to the wall to steady them both, drawing them nearer to the glowing lantern light.

"The surgeon's room is just there," Percy murmured. He gestured toward the doorway, his fingers trembling with nerves.

Heather gripped Percy's arm again, in an effort to maintain her footing, and they took the few steps into the surgeon's room.

Inside, a lantern swung wildly with the *Sapphire*'s motion, and the surgeon stood over a short box of corked bottles. The man was lean and bespectacled, with a full red beard, and he smiled at them upon their entrance.

"Ah! Ye've need o' me, aye?" The man's thick Scottish brogue rumbled in the small space, and Heather returned his smile.

Fucking hell. The side of her face was entirely covered in blood. It coated her hair and streaked her pale face.

"Good god, Heather! What happened?" he burst out.

She gave Percy a sidelong glance, but spoke to the surgeon. "Yes, sir. I have. I fell from bed and hit my head on the chest of drawers."

"Ach, aye. Come 'ere, then, lass." He gestured to a low cushioned bench along one side of the room, and she sat. "Tha' is a mighty bump."

"Yes, sir."

"Name's Duncan." He smiled again.

"I'm Heather Morgan."

Her gaze drifted past the surgeon toward where Percy hovered in the doorway. She looked as though she'd been through a battle, for Christ's sake. Her face, neck, and hands were entirely covered in crimson. But beneath it, she was pale.

"I didn't realize how much blood she'd lost," Percy said. "Will she be well, Duncan?"

"Ach, aye; 'ead wounds always bleed more 'n they should."

He wet a cloth from a pitcher and carefully removed the blood that covered her. With soft words of comfort, the man cleaned the area, prepared his needle, and stitched the small wound on her head.

The frigate continued to rock and tilt, the storm tossing

them about like a twig among rapids, the lantern swinging and the bottles on the surrounding shelves clinking as they hit the shelf rail. And yet Percy's attention was narrowed entirely on *her*.

"Have you anything for seasickness?" she asked softly.

"If I 'ad th' right herbs, I'd be able t' treat yer seasickness, but I'm nae an apothecary any longer, an' these men donnae get seasick, so I havenae wha's required." He clucked his tongue. "But I'll see ye patched up."

Interest brightened her gaze. "You were an apothecary?" she asked. "I confess, I've always been interested in the practice. Back home, I'd begun to collect plants based on their uses in apothecary, with the hopes of taking on the role in—" She shook her head slightly, cutting herself off. "What herbs do you require? I wasn't able to bring all of my plants aboard with me, but I do have several that might help."

"'Tis a noble endeavour, indeed." The man grinned at Heather, his red beard bunching. "I 'ave a small 'mount o' olive oil an' beeswax fer a salve, but I havenae any fennel seed or catnip."

Heather pulled her bottom lip between her teeth. "I have *Nepeta cataria* in the hold, but I haven't any *Foeniculum vulgare* seed. Does the plant require drying?"

Duncan's reply faded behind the rushing in Percy's ears. *Seasickness? Oh, hell.* He didn't know enough about pregnancy to know how soon a woman might feel ill after sex.

A cold sweat formed behind his knees and down his back.

His gaze sharpened on her as she spoke eagerly and animatedly with Duncan, and, despite himself, Percy felt a pang of longing in his chest alongside his trepidation. He wanted more of Heather's discussion, wanted the fiery passion in her gaze to be directed at *him*.

Her full, rosy mouth curved upward, and he remembered tasting those petal-soft lips. She'd been sodding delicious. *And look where it's gotten you*, his mind whispered.

Percy shifted his stance and gripped the door's frame as another swell hit the ship.

With an internal rebuke, he let his gaze roam over her. She was a mite pale, but that could be attributed to her injury. *Was it seasickness?*

"... And o' course," Duncan was saying, "ye and any other women on board may take these cloths any time tha' ye require 'em. I assure ye they're clean, and while I havenae the proper items required fer a young lass aboard the ship, these will do nicely, I believe."

"Thank you, sir. I—" The words died on Heather's tongue, her eyes glazing for a long moment before she blinked. "I'll let the other women know."

She smiled thinly before rising to her feet, gripping at the wall of shelves as the ship tilted. Thanking the surgeon once more, she made her way past Percy and into the narrow corridor. Percy saluted the man and walked with Heather in silence through the darkness, his mind abuzz and his stomach all but entirely in knots.

He wanted to offer her comfort, but the concept was so unfamiliar to him. His gut swooped, then flipped over with trepidation. He hadn't the faintest notion of how to inquire about a woman's courses...so he wouldn't. If she wanted to offer information, to confide in him, she would. He simply had to ensure she felt safe enough to talk to him.

"Seasickness, Heather?" he asked softly.

HER MIND awhirl and her stomach buzzing with nerves, Heather nodded. "Mmm," she hummed into the darkness.

The *Sapphire* pitched, and she flung out her arms, settling one hand on Percy's thickly muscled arm. Lord above, the man was large!

Her inner warnings to *release the man's arm* went unheeded as her grip lingered far longer than required. His radiating warmth seemed to travel up her arm and envelop her. A quivering heat spread through her stomach, and she leaned closer...before reason intervened, and she released him on a gasp.

For pity's sake, Heather!

She softly cleared her throat, suddenly very aware of the slumbering men around them on the mess deck. "My guard is gone tonight—no doubt due to the storm—but one is likely to take his place in the morn. We must quickly devise a plan to free me of their watchful eye so that I might speak privately with the captain. No doubt our good fortune will soon run its course and the earl will discover his missing documents. We haven't much time, Percy."

Light flashed through the companionway, followed swiftly by a crack of thunder.

"Yes, of course you're right," he muttered. "In addition to confining you, the earl has struck at my reputation—likely due to his suspicion about our acquaintance. For that reason, despite my efforts, I've not only been unable to speak with the captain, but I've also lost sway with the crew."

"Why would the captain and crew take the earl's word over yours?" she asked. "He's a fool."

Percy shrugged. "A powerful fool."

"What if I professed an emergency and sent my guard away?"

"That could work."

Her eyes widened as an idea struck. "What of right *now*?"

"The captain will be on the quarterdeck, manning the helm during the storm."

"Damn."

He huffed a laugh. "Your idea of an emergency on the

morrow is sound. Wait until the storm has passed, to ensure the captain has retreated once more to his cabin."

She deflated. "Very well."

He cleared his throat softly. "I shall leave you to your sleep. If you require any aid—any at all—I'm more than happy to provide it."

"Good night, Percy," she whispered.

His gaze scanned her features before he tugged on his forelock. "Sleep well, Heather." With that, he turned and strode back to the swinging hammocks, nearly disappearing in the dark.

Heather entered her diminutive cabin, gripping the wall and the chest of drawers as the ship tilted. Hell, but her *world* had tilted.

She lowered herself to the hanging bed, its rhythmic *clunk, thunk, clunk, thunk* joining the thudding pulse in her ears.

For the briefest of moments with the surgeon, she'd thought it possible that she could be pregnant. *Heaven forfend!*

Her courses had been meant to arrive within the first few days that she'd been aboard. That window had come to a close more than a sennight ago. Just as quickly as her worry had come, however, it had fled. She recalled seeing spots of blood. Not her ordinary menses, to be sure, but mayhap the strain of the journey had caused the irregularity. It was entirely plausible.

She pulled her lips between her teeth and worried the delicate flesh.

Clunk, thunk, clunk...thunk. Her bed continued to beat a rhythmic tattoo between the wall and chest of drawers, while her heart thrummed with anxiety and her stomach swirled with nausea.

CHAPTER 8

Warm wind whipped at the hem of Percy's ill-fitting blue coat as he adjusted the lines. His feet were braced apart, keeping him balanced as the ship gently rocked on the calmed morning water. He'd scarcely slept after returning Heather to her cabin, his mind racing and his ears filled with his neighbour's ungodly snoring.

He'd listened for any sign of movement from the woman's cabin, ready to leap to her aid should she require it. But she'd remained abed. Then his thoughts had drifted to their tryst in the gazebo: how she'd moved, how she'd tasted, and, *Christ*, the sounds she'd made...

Clearing his throat, he focused on the topman in the rigging above him and adjusted the lines.

"*No, damn it*," the earl shouted across the *Sapphire*'s quarterdeck. "I asked for *port*. This is sodding Madeira!"

The noise drew Percy's gaze. The Earl of Hanley was flapping a hand at one of the footmen he'd brought aboard, and the man of middling years flushed red to the tips of his ears before bowing and scurrying away. Percy frowned. He could scarcely wait to see the blackguard tossed in the brig.

Speaking of the brig…

Squinting through the sunlight, Percy scanned the quarterdeck for any sign of Heather. *Damnation.* Mayhap her guard hadn't believed her plea.

Maybe she's ill due to pregnancy, his inner fear whispered.

Alarm spread across his chest and down the backs of his legs, and, abruptly, he needed to see her.

With a shout over his shoulder, he called the attention of another man, who approached at a trot.

"Have to piss," Percy said crassly, and the man nodded, accepting the lines.

Instead of turning toward the head—the seat of easement for the crew—Percy spun on his heel and hurried belowdecks. As he descended the last rung to the gun deck, he noted one of the earl's maids—whom he'd frequently seen aiding in preparing meals for the crew—leaving Heather's cabin, her arms laden with a chamber pot and soiled rags.

Holy hell. His stomach all but sank through the frigate and into the ocean below them. He darted toward her open doorway.

"Heather?" he inquired cautiously, his voice rough.

She was sitting sideways upon her bed, resting against the wall with her knees brought up to her chest, her lilac walking dress tucked snugly beneath her. Her pale skin glistened with perspiration, and her red-blonde locks were unruly and sticking to her forehead, cheeks, and neck. But the moment her eyes met his, her nearly colourless lips curved upward in a half smile, and his chest constricted. She beckoned him forward.

"Hell's teeth, Heather," he breathed, coming closer. "Are you well? Has the surgeon been to see you?"

Her lips thinned, and her gaze slid past him before meeting his once more. "He has."

And? His heart constricted.

She patted the space beside her on the bed with one hand, and he sat.

"And what of the salve, or whatever Duncan had said of that remedy for seasickness?"

"I..." Her voice was hoarse, her eyes glistening. "I'm afraid my *Nepeta cataria*—the catnip plant—has perished in the hold while I've been...*imprisoned*. In fact, nearly a third of my plants—" A sob caught in her throat, and Percy's heart gave a sharp pang. "Never mind. Fresh air, the doctor says, and some buns ought to settle my stomach. But the earl won't allow it."

Percy frowned. "Won't *allow* it?"

She swiped at her eyes with the back of one hand and sniffled. "He thoroughly outlined his displeasure with my appear —" With a twisted grimace, Heather gathered the fresh chamber pot sitting beside her and retched.

Another wave of worry and fear rippled through him. He wanted to put a hand to her back in a comforting gesture, but he'd heard from men at the pugilists' club that some women— the men's wives, in particular—despised being touched while being ill. And Percy didn't wish to impose himself on Heather without her permission. He did, however, accept a clean chamber pot from the maid as the woman returned, and he dampened a cloth for Heather to use for her forehead, neck, or mouth, as she chose.

The small space echoed with the wretched sounds of heaving, and Percy's gut knotted in sympathy. At last, she rinsed and wiped her mouth, then sat back against the wall.

"Thank you, Berta," Heather murmured with a half-hearted smile toward the maid.

"O'course, miss." The maid reached forward and withdrew the used chamber pot with a lingering sideways glance at Percy before she retreated.

"Feeling any better?" Percy asked softly, not knowing how else to offer comfort in such a moment.

Heather took a stuttered breath and nodded slightly. "Fractionally." Her eyes slid closed. "I owe you my thanks, as well, Percy."

"I—of course," he returned, nonplussed. "You're welcome."

A series of loud shouts rose up above them, followed closely by the sharp ringing of the bell. Heather flinched, and Percy shot to his feet.

"*Prepare for battle*!" a voice bellowed.

Percy froze.

Impossible. How had a ship come upon them so quickly? A chase often lasted hours, even days. Surely a topman would have noticed long before now that a ship was in pursuit.

"*Run out the guns*!" someone shouted.

"*Hell*," Percy breathed. "Something isn't right. I have to go." He turned to Heather, his tone urgent. "Remain hidden. Bar the door behind me, and do not open it for anyone."

And with that, he left, closing the door on the woman who could be carrying his child.

On the mess deck, the night shift of men scrambled to ready themselves for battle, some still dressed. Some ran belowdecks toward the magazine, while others darted above. Percy ascended to the gun deck, where the cannons and carronades were being run out, and his gut knotted.

What the devil am I doing? Heat spread across his chest, and nerves twisted inside him. He ought to be with Heather, not leaving her to hide. What would he do should the *Sapphire* be boarded? What if he was engaged above deck and something happened to Heather? She'd begun her training, but she was by no means an experienced fighter.

Two men jostled him as they hurried past, and Percy blinked. *Ballocks*. He turned on his heel to return belowdecks when an officer appeared before him.

"To your duties, linesman," the officer grunted, thrusting

a water-filled bucket and a French cutlass at him, his eyes creased with poorly disguised trepidation. "Pirates are approaching. Fast."

THE SMALL CABIN echoed with the sound of Heather's agitated breathing, men shouting, footfalls overhead, and the rushing of her pulse in her ears. Had the maids been ushered to an officer's cabin, or had they been sent to the hold? The Earl of Shite had undoubtedly commandeered the captain's cabin in which to hide, and demanded his men stand as personal protection. The bloody coward.

Oh, blast, her plants! The surviving plants were in the hold. She hoped no harm came to them during the battle.

More shouts rose up overhead, and nausea churned in Heather's stomach. Aware that she might soon be required to flee—and abhorring the metallic tang on her tongue—she hastily retrieved her tooth powder and toothbrush and set to cleaning her mouth.

Battle. The word whispered through her mind as she brushed.

Footfalls raced back and forth, followed by heavy thuds. *Are those bodies or cannonballs?* She loathed not knowing what was happening and not being able to help.

A detestable sense of helplessness stole over her, and she retreated once more to her swinging bed.

Boom! Her cabin vibrated with the first blast of a cannon, and, for the first time, a tremor of fear shot through her nerves.

Battle. It wasn't just between the men, it was between the sodding ships. But what of the ship meant to be sailing behind the *Sapphire*? There was no way of knowing if they'd encountered these attackers first, or if the attackers approached from another direction. If their partnered ship hadn't been attacked, surely they would soon come upon them and offer their aid. Two ships against one would see them to victory against these aggressors.

Boom-boom! Two more blasts, followed closely by the bellows of men. Heather's breath caught.

Pulling her legs to her breasts, she trained her ears above her, listening to every movement and wondering if Percy was all right.

Boom...boom...boom...

"READY TO TURN, LADS!" the officer said.

Percy tugged on his forelock and obeyed the order, set to line up the ship in preparation for battle. He pulled on the halyard, keeping the rope taut and awaiting his next command. But despite the overwrought air surrounding him, his gaze drifted to the companionway.

Was Heather still unwell? Was she frightened? Hell, he ought to have defied orders and returned to her cabin to be with her.

"*Turn!*" the officer shouted, as the topmen worked and gunners scrambled along the deck, preparing the cannons.

Avoiding being cut by the French cutlass tucked into his newly found belt, Percy heaved hard on the halyard, his hands fisting one over the other as he pulled. The rope reached its end, and he swiftly tied it off at the main jeer-bitts.

"Ready, men! *Aim!*" their captain hollered from the helm.

Christ, this was it. Percy turned from his task, his heart in his throat.

"*Fire!*"

Boom! The explosion reverberated through his chest, which swelled with...hell, was that anticipation? He hadn't engaged in battle in some time, and while he was terrified for Heather, part of him was desirous for a fight.

Boom-boom! One of the *Sapphire*'s cannons fired, just as their opponent drew alongside them and fired theirs, the ball sailing through the air not far from Percy to glance off the far taffrail. Hell, that had been close.

A row of men stepped up to the bulwark between the cannons and carronades and lifted muskets to their shoulders, aiming at the opposing ship. Above him, the marksmen on the fighting tops took aim as well.

"*Fire at will!*" the captain called.

Crack-crack-crack-crack!

More gunpowder filled the air, shaking Percy from his momentary immobility. He'd been in countless battles before. But while there might be more at stake for him now, he knew how to fight, and he bloody well knew how to win.

Boom...boom...boom...

The *Sapphire* shook with the force of the cannon fire, and a ball sailed through the air to splinter the mizzen topgallant mast. Percy darted sideways as several topmen leapt for the shrouds, clinging for life to the ladder-like ropes, while a few others fell to their doom. *Fuck.*

Withdrawing his French cutlass, Percy hurried to the bulwark, where the men were either reloading the carronades and their muskets or preparing the planks to board the other ship. That's what Percy was waiting for, *that* was when he would excel, his—

All thought ceased as a wicked, keening laughter cut through the cacophony of noise. *Hell's tits*, he knew that laugh. He'd heard it before, many times...for it was the sound of his nightmares.

Breath caught in his throat and his pulse fluttered like a sodding butterfly as he scanned their opponent's ship. He knew what he'd see, and still he froze at the sight of the enormous Scotsman, his wild, greying red hair and beard visible even through the haze of gunpowder. Sunlight glinted off the insignia on the man's pilfered Redcoat and, his experience notwithstanding, a tremor stole over Percy's body.

The Butcher.

CHAPTER 9

*B*efore he realized that he'd moved, Percy's feet had carried him through the throng of terrified men and down the companionway to the gun deck. It mightn't have registered in his mind yet, but his heart and body damned well knew what to do: reach Heather and get her to Butcher's ship.

Boom! Boom-boom! The frigate shook, and men hollered. The scent of perspiration, gunpowder, and fear permeated the air, and Percy kept going.

No ship that Butcher came across was ever left sailing. No man was ever left alive. The man was his namesake: a butcher. And if Percy did not get Heather off the *Sapphire*, she would perish as well.

His feet drummed against the tar-sealed wood planks of the deck before he descended the next companionway and ran to Heather's cabin. Skidding to a halt, he lifted a trembling hand to knock, and swallowed the bile that had risen to his throat.

There was only one option for him, and—*Christ alive*—he hated it. He would do whatever it took to protect Heather from harm, however, and if his plan had the benefit of keeping more of this crew alive, then it was best.

He licked his dry lips. "Heather, it's me."

STARS SPARKED behind Heather's eyelids as she rubbed at the dratted prickling that wouldn't abate. She detested feeling helpless, and while tears were a good release, they gave her the headache and wouldn't do her any good at the moment.

She took a deep breath and rested her chin upon her knees once more, listening to the thundering of footfalls, the shouts, and the rumble of gunfire. Tossing aside the lilac muslin of her skirts, she reached for her mother's journal in her uppermost drawer and hugged it to her chest. She mightn't be able to read it in the darkness of the room, but she took comfort in its nearness. And, of course, it contained those important pilfered documents...

She squeezed her eyelids shut and thought back to the masquerade...

Knock-knock, knock-knock.

Heather's spine straightened. Who would be knocking on her door in the middle of a battle?

"Heather, it's me."

Percy. Her breath left her in a relieved whoosh, and she rushed from the bed to unbolt the door. The scent of gunpowder and perspiration confronted her as she swung it open.

The brief moment of relief that washed over her fled immediately at the sight of him. His usually pink-flushed and sun-kissed skin was pale and sweat-slickened. His hair was wild, and his dark eyes were full of...*Lord,* was it fear?

"We have to go," he burst out.

Boom! The *Sapphire* shook, and cries rang out above them, sending a shiver down Heather's spine.

"*Go?*" She blinked. "Do you mean *fight*? I haven't a weapon, but I am willing to—"

He shook his head sharply and clasped her hand in his. "Off the ship."

Boom-boom.

"*Pardon*? What of the others? What of Berta?" Her heart squeezed. "And my plants!"

"I'm afraid we haven't time." He cut a glance at her and took her mother's journal from her numb fingers. "Please trust me, Heather."

And she did.

Percy tugged on her hand, and in a momentary panic, Heather reached out with her free arm and grabbed one of the potted plants that sat upon her chest of drawers, the minty horehound leaves shaking with the movement. She couldn't very well leave without at least *trying* to save one.

Percy tutted softly and shook his head, but he led her through the nearly abandoned mess deck—where he retrieved a satchel in which to stow the journal—and up the companionway onto the gun deck.

Boom!

An involuntary curse escaped Heather as the cannon fire reverberated through her chest. She hesitated while men scurried about, loading the cannons and preparing the ammunition. But she hadn't long to look, for Percy pulled her toward the next companionway.

Boom—crack! Fear sizzled along her skin and hastened her steps as the wall behind them splintered, spraying shards of wood through the air and sending a man sailing past on a hoarse cry.

"*My god,*" Heather breathed.

Percy tightened his hold on her hand. "Butcher will leave no one left alive."

"*Butcher?*"

He nodded brusquely. "The captain. The damned thing is that his pirates are capable of being decent men, but they're tempted by greed, bound by duty, and ruled by fear. And Butcher is not one to forgive; he will kill any man who defies him."

"How do you know all of this?"

They ascended hastily to the quarterdeck, where—*blimey*—hand-to-hand combat had broken out.

Percy's lips tightened as he took in the crush of pirates running across wooden planks that now connected the two ships. Others swung down onto the deck from ropes. The thudding of footfalls, the cries of pain, the clangs of swords and cutlasses, the splashing of the ocean, and the occasional crack of a pistol filled her ears. Gentle wind swirled past, carrying with it the scent of gunpowder, sweat, and the metallic zing of blood.

Heather tamped down her nausea. She wanted to pursue the matter of the man called Butcher, but this was most certainly not the time.

"We will need to fight our way through," Percy said over his shoulder as he shifted his satchel.

He led them forward, then paused to retrieve something from the ground, and Heather's hold tightened instinctively around her plant.

Boom-boom-boom!

She flinched as the ship trembled beneath her feet.

And, slowly, they moved. Men jostled around them as Percy swung his cutlass and cleared their path.

A shout and a sickening gurgle came from beside them, before one of their crew fell at their feet with a hollow *thud*.

The pirate standing behind him whooped triumphantly before he rushed toward Heather.

Oh, ballocks. Another man leapt upon Percy, leaving her alone with her pirate, and despite her hours of training, her instincts took over.

With a screech, she lifted the plant high above her head and swung it downward. It connected with the pirate's temple with a solid clunk. The man toppled to the deck, dirt and shattered earthenware spread over him.

"Capital hit," Percy said beside her, his breath coming hard as he stepped over his own opponent, who was sprawled beside Heather's.

"Thank you," she breathed, remorse coursing through her. "That was my *Marrubium vulgare.*"

Percy gripped her wrist and placed the handle of a long-bladed dagger against her palm, his dark eyes solemn. "Keep this dirk on your person. Stab any man who comes close. You remember your training?"

Boom! The *Sapphire* shook beneath her.

"I do." She nodded, her gaze darting around. Blood splattered her skirts from two men fighting nearby, and she grimaced.

"Good." Percy gripped her free hand in his, the heat of his palm sending a spark of awareness up her arm, despite the utterly inopportune time. "Remain close."

With that, he turned back into the fray, leading her along behind him. *Blimey,* this was it. She was in a proper battle, expected to do harm with an actual sodding weapon, not their wooden practice ones. But she didn't know enough to survive in a battle such as this! Did she?

Fear and anxiety travelled in waves throughout her body, trembling in her fingers and twisting in her stomach, but she followed Percy. She trusted him.

Ahead of her, he was meeting opponent after opponent

with his cutlass, smoothly slicing his blade through the air and across their flesh as though he had been born to it.

They reached the bulwark where two long wooden planks precariously connected the ships. *Lord above, does he expect me to walk across that?*

"We must cross," he said, confirming her fears as he wiped his perspiring brow with his sleeve.

Boom-boom!

A beast of a man launched himself at Percy, and he grunted at the impact, working quickly to fight him off.

A flash of movement to her right caught her eye, and instinct once again took over. She arched her arm high, swinging the dirk through the air at the approaching figure. Her heart thundered, rushing in her ears and hammering in her throat. But the man stopped, his eyes wild on her as he licked his lips.

"I like 'em fiery," he growled lasciviously. His gaze raked over her, and she shivered with revulsion. "I'll take ye right 'ere."

He lunged.

"*No!*" Percy hollered, as another opponent tackled him from the side.

Horror nearly froze her, but she tightened her grip on the dirk and brought the blade swiftly up between them, its tip digging shallowly into the blackguard's jugular and halting the man's forward motion. He glared at her, his heavy, fetid breath wafting over her cheeks and ruffling her hair.

"You will not have me," she said, astonished at the calm that had settled over her.

Despite the upheaval around her, and the slight churn in her stomach, her body knew what to do, knew how to react. And if this was how she would survive, then she would do as she must.

P ULSE THUNDERING, Percy punched the hilt of his cutlass into his opponent's eye, felling the man with a choked scream. Then he turned toward Heather. There she stood, her eyes steely as she glared at the pirate before her, her blade at the man's throat.

His pulse fluttered, and his cock gave a twitch of acknowledgement. *Damn*, but she was beautiful.

"Step back and let us pass," she said coolly.

The cur did as he was told, his eyes flashing with both hate and fear. Agonized cries rose around them, and all at once Percy lost his patience. The crew was dying, for fuck's sake. They hadn't time to waste.

He stepped forward and rapped the hilt of his cutlass across the man's skull with a solid thunk, knocking the man out.

"Percy!" she breathed, her gaze wide on him. "Have you been hurt?"

He blinked, and with a grunt and a grimace of realization, he swiped at his face with the sleeve of his coat before pulling the irksome thing from his shoulders and dropping it to the deck. He was too bloody hot, anyway...and he knew what must happen for his plan to succeed. "No, I am well. I was bled upon." He gripped her hand once more. "You did excellent. Are you well enough to continue?"

A small smile curved her lips. "Of course."

He nodded. "Keep the dirk at the ready."

Boom!

With that, they skirted past a fighting trio of men—one of whom was Stubbs—and across the planks connecting the ships. Fewer men were aboard the pirate's ship, but while he was grateful for fewer potential threats against Heather, it also meant that they were easier to see coming.

"Someone's gutted the captain!" one of the naval officers screamed.

More shouts and shrieks rent the air as the naval crew flew into a panic.

There was no hope for it. He spun his head to shout at her over his shoulder. "*Run!*"

His palm tight against hers, Percy ran, cutting down any pirate who dared get in his path. Butcher stood against the bulwark at the fo'c'sle, his broad back to them. He couldn't hesitate. He had one chance to make this plan work, or they were all dead, Heather—and perhaps his unborn babe—included.

Fuck. His gut twisted. Heather was going to hate him.

On swift feet they neared Butcher, and Percy set his plan into action. In a smooth series of movements, he released Heather's hand to retrieve the blunderbuss he'd tucked into his slops, then tossed his satchel to the deck. Without a moment's hesitation, he swept forward to tuck his blade beneath Butcher's chin and his blunderbuss to the bastard's temple, the man well and truly caught.

He sucked in a deep breath and let out a shrill whistle, garnering the attention of the men directly around them. "*Ring the bell,*" Percy bellowed.

A growl went through Butcher, his body taut as a bowstring and veritably vibrating with the force of his fury. "I know you," he rumbled.

Percy ignored the bastard, feeling the other pirates' gazes burning into his back. But they didn't dare interfere when their captain's life was in Percy's hands.

Bong, bong, bong, bong. The bell rang, and the sounds of battle subsided as all eyes turned Percy's way. *No hesitation.*

Percy's grip tightened on the blunderbuss as Butcher gripped his shirtfront.

Bang!

Percy pulled the trigger, the blunderbuss backfiring in his hand with a flash of light. But Butcher went down. His head whipped sideways, propelling his body overboard and tearing Percy's ill-fitting shirt from his frame. Percy let him fall to the ocean with a heavy splash, while he remained on board, entirely bare-chested.

Fuck.

A low murmur went through the conscious men, while those nearby took several steps back.

"There will be no more fighting!" Percy hollered, his voice carrying. He gritted his teeth against the surge of fear and trepidation that threatened to overtake him at what he knew must come next. "Some of you know me. But for those of you who do not, I am Percival Baxter, and I am taking over this ship."

CHAPTER 10

It's him.

Heather's heart slammed against her ribs, her pulse drumming in her ears and throbbing at her throat as she stared at Percy's bared skin.

It may have been dark, but she'd seen those tattoos before —the anchor and rope that stretched across his broad, muscular chest and abdomen, surrounded by swallows in flight. And when he'd turned around that night, the moonlight had clearly delineated a skull and bones, inked over the entirety of his back... Indeed, she would recognize them anywhere.

Heat suffused her cheeks, even while a cold chill raced down her spine. Did Percy *know*? If he didn't, surely she must tell him... Her heart hiccoughed, and her stomach grew fraught with nerves.

Hell's teeth, she'd had sex with Percy.

As though he'd heard her thoughts, his gaze swung to meet hers over his shoulder. And it was there, in the heat of his dark glance, the way his gaze dipped to her toes and raked up her body, as though seeing through her clothes to the blushing skin beneath. *The cad.* Her inner muscles clenched as though in memory of their tryst, and she cursed her body's reaction.

The blackguard had known all this time, and he'd said nothing to her! While the opportunities hadn't been plentiful, they'd spoken privately several times over the past weeks, and yet he'd said naught. *Why?*

He broke their heated stare with a wink, and to Heather's irritation, warmth gathered at the apex of her thighs. To her credit, the man was decidedly stunning in the midday sun, his suntanned skin glistening from the exertion of battle and his muscles bunched with tension, as though prepared for attack. *Blimey.*

No, Heather! He lied to you, drat it.

Indeed. She ought to be displeased. A sigh escaped her, and the tension that had suddenly gathered in her shoulders eased a little. His revealing the truth would have served little purpose. She'd gotten what she'd wanted: an anonymous tryst at a masquerade.

"Now—and only now—will I give you a choice," Percy boomed. "The pirates that don't wish to sail under my command may leave. And any of Sir Willard's crew that wish to join mine may do so now."

Both crews were captivated by Percy's speech, their eyes wide with a mix of astonishment and horror. He'd implied the men would know him as Percival Baxter, and while she'd been made aware of his prior position at sea, Heather failed to comprehend the significance of the announcement.

There was a low murmur from the men before Percy's voice cut it off. "*But*...if I hear even a breath of mutiny, I'll slit your fucking throats."

A shiver raced up Heather's spine despite the heat of the sun.

Many of the earl's men and the naval crew had perished or been gravely injured in battle. They neither had a captain nor a first mate, and those who remained were outnumbered and overwhelmed. Heather's stomach gave another sharp twist. So many lives lost.

"*Make your choice*!" Percy hollered. "And when you have, go down to the hold and retrieve their stores. They have another ship coming with additional supplies." He paused. "And do not forget the plants! But, for Lucifer's sake, be careful with them."

To her amazement, men—even several members of the other crew—began shuffling toward the companionway on the other ship.

"What in the bloody hell is this?" The earl emerged from the companionway, his eyes narrowed and blinking. He took in the bodies and blood, and his features grew yet more stormy.

One of the surviving officers stepped forward and informed him of what just transpired.

The earl's outraged glare swung toward Heather and intensified. "I should think *not*! Return to the *Sapphire* at once! These men will handle matters. We've another frigate on the way." His voice carried across the narrow distance between the two ships, and Heather's abdomen quivered instinctively in response.

"And I'll not have our stores emptied, blast it!" the earl blustered.

"You haven't the choice," Percy called to the man. "You've no need of such largesse, and if your remaining crew wish to join me, then so must their share of your hold."

The Earl of Shite's face reddened in his fury. "Who are you to speak to me in this way, to demand these things? I ought to—"

"Percival Baxter," Percy said from beside her.

Shock jolted through Heather as the earl's complexion grew pallid. He turned his fearful gaze on her.

"Come with me this instant, Calluna," he said, with a quaver to his voice.

What am I missing?

Heather shook herself. Swift thinking and decisiveness were required of her, so she'd best not tarry. Thus far she'd been unsuccessful in apprehending the earl. No path before her would see her fulfilling her assignment directly or easily.

If she remained with the earl, she would undoubtedly be imprisoned on the other frigate, which would see her to the Americas to be wed to the bastard before she returned to England to present her evidence against him—all without Percy's aid.

She could impress upon Percy the importance of taking the earl with them and holding him in the brig. But that would likely see them pursued across the ocean by the captain of the following ship—and very possibly yet *more* navy frigates geared and ready to engage in battle. Why, the earl himself had boasted about a member of the royal family arranging his safe passage. Until Heather could provide proof of treason, the earl was protected. And his royal connection no doubt harboured a special interest in the security of those documents. Alas, the man to whom she would have presented the proof was now deceased.

Another—and decidedly more appealing—option was to simply join Percy on the pirate ship in the hope that she could hasten back home. Exposing the earl's treason before he returned from the Americas would allow time for the magistrate and his men to prepare for the earl's capture upon reaching the Pool of London.

First, however, she must ensure that her ties to the earl as his affianced were severed. A comfortable solution, that would both see her securely away from the earl and dissuade the pirates from pursuing her, appeared in her mind with complete clarity.

Low groaning came from a number of the injured men on the *Sapphire*, but their cries and pleas went unheeded.

She stepped closer to the bulwark as a gust of warm wind ruffled her hair and tugged at her bloodstained skirts. "*No.* I cannot marry you."

The earl's face reddened once more, and he clenched his fists. "You will do so, or I shall tell your family what you've done. I shall inform the *ton*! You will be disgraced! You will—"

Heather's body moved before she could think better of it. She pivoted on the ball of one foot and pulled Percy into her arms. He gave a surprised grunt as she pressed her body flush against his, surged up on her toes, and took his lips with hers.

DELICIOUS HEAT TINGLED down Percy's spine to curve snugly around his cods as Heather wrapped herself around him. Her tongue gently prodded his lips, and he opened eagerly for her, returning the kiss with fervour.

His hands fisted the material of her frock, pulling her tighter against him. His pulse sped as their tongues clashed. A moan escaped her, and she thrust her hips against his hardening cock. A responding groan vibrated in his chest.

But just as quickly as the kiss began, it ended, leaving him winded and entirely bemused.

He blinked dazedly at her before she gave him a wink and turned to face her intended. *Fuck.* Percy wanted her to do that again but in a decidedly more private locale. Christ knew what message such a display had sent to the pirates about her potential availability. He couldn't let that stand.

"*I shall not be made a cuckold*! Get back to this ship right now, Calluna! I have our marriage licence. I could have the captain—er, the *other* captain—marry us directly!" the earl shouted, his wrinkled face turning purple in his outrage.

Percy put a hand to her back and brushed his lips to her ear, ignoring the flutter of his pulse. "Stand firm. You're doing well, Heather."

"We mustn't bring him with us and risk pursuit," she whispered back. "If we reach London before the earl—"

"Yes," he said. "But first, I must secure my place among these men or risk murder or mutiny. And we need to establish your character as one on which these pirates mustn't prey."

Satisfied by her small nod, Percy resumed his focus on the *Sapphire*.

"This is mutiny!" the earl blustered, as men marched past, their arms laden with items from the hold. "Put that back! Those are my—"

Percy'd had enough. "Bind the earl," he called. "Be sure to clear the magazine and armoury, but leave the earl's wardrobe. Collect abandoned weaponry and ammunition and, for God's sake, raid the cabins."

He couldn't risk the earl knowing the documents were on the pirate ship, or hell would be on their tails. The blackguard's wardrobe—crates of boots included—*must* remain with the earl.

"Aye, Cap'n," several of the pirates replied in chorus.

A jolt of pride, followed by a swift thread of panic, burst behind Percy's ribs, and he gritted his teeth and nodded. He couldn't—bloody well *couldn't*—be pulled into the ocean life again, regardless of how the pirates' piety made him feel.

I killed Butcher. The panic in his chest swelled. *Fuck*.

"Y'want us t'kill 'im, Cap'n?" one of the crew asked.

Percy gave a sharp shake of his head. "No. That won't be necessary." He wasn't the pirate they thought he was. Not anymore.

A noise of agitation came from beside him, and Percy turned toward the source. Heather's gaze was fixed on the

Sapphire, her brow furrowed in concern and her bottom lip pulled between her teeth.

He followed her line of sight to several pirates carrying wilting potted plants across the deck. They were in a sorry state, indeed.

"What environment would be best for their revival?" he asked in an undertone.

Her pained green gaze flicked upward to meet his. "Partial sunlight and fresh water."

He nodded, then called to the men carrying the pots. "Put the plants in my cabin."

STEADFASTLY RESISTING the urge to press herself into Percy's side as the pirates passed with items from the *Sapphire*, Heather focused instead on the warmth spreading through her chest. Even while he was embroiled in piracy politics that were beyond her understanding—*Was he truly the captain of the pirates simply because he killed that Butcher fellow? Did the position not fall to the next in line?*—Percy had considered the well-being of her plants.

"Thank you," she said softly.

He gave another nod, his gaze still on the trussing of the earl. They'd gagged him as well, but his face had grown so alarmingly purple it appeared about to burst.

"Look wha' we found quiverin' in th' 'old!" one of the pirates exclaimed, dragging a tearful Berta out of the companionway.

Percy stiffened beside her, and Heather's breath caught in her throat. *No!* Berta couldn't be caught—she wouldn't be safe among the pirates!

"No," Heather whispered. "No, Percy, they can't."

"*Leave her and the other women!*" Percy bellowed. "Do as

you're told, or you'll join the dead when we give them their sea burial."

The men worked quickly and efficiently, gathering items from the *Sapphire* and bringing them aboard the pirate ship, and Heather couldn't help but notice the stares the pirates gave Percy as they passed. To her astonishment, they watched him with not only wariness but...*awe*. It made her wish she shared their knowledge.

"Percival," said a low voice behind them.

Percy whirled and blinked, first in confusion and then in shock, as he took in the man before them.

"Hell's tits, Donovan!" His teeth gleamed in a broad smile as he clasped the pirate's large hand and shook it.

"It's bloody good to see you, friend." The wide man nodded vigorously and smiled, revealing only slightly yellowed teeth in return.

The pirate was nearly as tall as Percy, though he had more breadth, and where Percy's smooth, slightly tanned skin glowed rosy in the sunlight, Mr. Donovan's was a deep, glorious mahogany that seemed to absorb the sun. They grinned at each other, but while their dark gazes locked, Heather sensed that a wealth of unspoken words passed between them.

At last, Percy cleared his throat. "Heather, this is Donovan. I've known him since boyhood. Donovan, this is Miss Morgan, a fearsome and highly respected runner from London."

Another burst of warmth flared in Heather's chest as she greeted the pirate. He ducked his head, his eyes curious and also filled with what seemed to Heather like profound sadness, and perhaps relief.

"What in Christ's name are you doing on Butcher's ship, Donovan?" Percy asked in an undertone.

"There's a few of us from them years on board. Ye'll see

the others soon, I wager." The man's smile slipped, and he glanced over his shoulder. "There ain't many options for pirates, as there ain't many of us left. Butcher was a bastard—most o' the crew hated him, and others wanted t' kill him—but he kept our necks from the noose."

Percy clapped his old friend on the shoulder, his lips tight and eyes troubled. "I understand. I should like to discuss this in greater detail later on. But Donovan...will you be my second-in-command?"

"Oh!" Donovan's eyes lit. "Aye, Percival—I-I mean Captain. Aye!"

"Very good. We must prepare to set sail. I tossed a satchel aside earlier—bring it to my cabin. Heather"—he turned to face her—"do keep your dirk at hand. These men are not to be trusted."

A jolt of nerves jumped through her abdomen, but she nodded her understanding.

He leaned close and whispered in her ear, "Remember your training. You have the skills. You are strong, capable, and damnably formidable when you put your mind to it."

Then he was gone. And her pulse was thundering.

HOLY HELL, what am I doing? Percy's gut twisted as he ordered the pirates about.

"Hoist the sails!" he called. "Scrub the deck!"

The bodies had already been thrown overboard, but blood remained. Luckily, most of the carnage had been sustained on the *Sapphire*, so there was less to clean. Additionally, Percy had to arrange for a thorough inspection of what was damaged during the battle. Lord knew the *Sapphire* wouldn't sail again, for its main mast had been downed, but although this ship was able to sail, it had borne damage.

His gaze swung toward Heather, who stood next to the bulwark at the aft end of the fo'c'sle, her elbow resting upon the taffrail and the wind blowing through her red-blonde tresses. He wanted to trace the sun's path across the bridge of her nose and over her cheekbones, to kiss away the pucker of a frown from between her brows.

He leaned against the starboard taffrail, attempting to better glimpse her features, but from that distance, it proved a challenge.

Hell. Was she pregnant with his child? The rush of seawater and wind filled his ears as his extremities grew numb despite the warmth of the day.

"Fuck," he muttered under his breath.

Despite his fears, imposing his ill pedigree—or lack thereof—on anyone was the least of his current concerns. He'd just felled *Butcher*, for Christ's sake! He'd taken on the role of sodding pirate captain, once more breaking a vow he'd sworn to uphold. And in doing so, he risked breaking another promise: keeping Heather safe.

His gaze slid her way again, and his gut clenched. Taking on the role of a member of the crew had been necessary...but so had *this*. Icy fear crept up his spine and flapped helplessly in his heart. As much as he despised even sniffing around his old life, he would take that leap again to keep Heather alive. For fuck knew they'd just landed in a tornado of shite and death.

And—*sodding hell*—how was he to return them to England? He couldn't risk sailing a pirate ship into the Pool of London, lest he risk not only his and the crew's necks but Heather's as well. This would bear ruminating on, for certain.

Christ, he ought to speak with Heather on the matter.

A gust of warm wind rushed past him, and his gaze lifted toward the darkening sky. He must spend time working on navigation, on planning. Never would he have guessed that he'd again require that particular skill. Indeed, he'd imagined himself working for the women on Bow Street, training and sparring while earning a small wage—for he certainly didn't require a larger one—and living out his life quietly.

"Captain Percival!"

Percy whirled at the voice, and smiled as Donovan approached. It was bloody good to see an old friend. But with that joy came fear...and *guilt*.

"Yes, Donovan?"

"We're sea ready. The men belowdecks are accommodating the new crew members and assessing the damage."

Percy nodded. "Excellent."

"We are well enough away from the *Sapphire*, Percival. You are free to make your announcement."

"Very good." Percy cleared his throat, inwardly cursing the sudden quiver of nerves in his abdomen. He jutted his chin toward the belfry. "Ring the bell."

CHAPTER 11

The once glistening surface of the water had grown muted, and the sky was a furious shade of grey. Percy eyed Heather beside him. She was blinking against the sharp turn of the wind as it pulled more of her hair free from its pins to blow wildly in front of her face. A lock caught on her lip, and she absently curled it behind her ear. His gut flipped.

Bong, bong, bong, bong.

This is it. Percy took a slow, deep breath through his nose in an attempt to calm his riotous nerves. But all the while, he was exceedingly aware of Heather's presence at his side. Before this assignment, they'd known each other well enough as an instructor and student, as friends, and even—after the masque—as lovers. *This*, however, was so much...more. With every truth, every revelation of his life, his very identity, left him feeling *exposed*.

Beside him, Heather gave an excited gasp, then leaned in close to Percy. "Duncan the surgeon came aboard!"

Grateful for the small diversion, he followed her line of

sight. "Delightful. Now you may discuss the apothecary and plants with someone who has knowledge of it."

Her smile fairly glowed with zeal, and a responding quiver jolted through Percy. Seeing her happy brought a new sort of pleasure he'd not expected. That bore further rumination, but now was decidedly not the time.

A muscle twitched in Percy's jaw as he eyed the crew gathered before him.

"*Men!*" Percy boomed, his arms held aloft as he addressed the crush. "As you've no doubt noticed, I selected my second in command: Donovan." The pirates murmured as Donovan inclined his head.

"I see some familiar faces among the crowd, but many that I don't yet know," Percy continued, his gut flipping again. *What must Heather think of me?* "I'm aware of the notoriety of my name, and while it mightn't carry the same influence as 'Butcher,' you'll be just as respected by the world as members of my crew. I shall ensure that you're fed, paid, and feared, precisely as a pirate ought to be. And I *will* keep you from the noose. But do not mistake my generosity for weakness. I mightn't be the sort of man to murder you while you sleep, but if you openly defy me, I'll keelhaul you."

His pulse skittered as another wave of fear danced up his spine. While he could engage in combat with these men individually, he was greatly outnumbered. If anyone chose to form a mutiny, or if—perish the thought—one or more of the men attempted to harm Heather...

He cleared his throat of the thickness that had settled there. "That brings me to my companion. The fearsome Miss Morgan is not here for your enjoyment." A chorus of groans swept the crew, and Percy resisted the possessive snarl that threatened. "As a deadly runner sent on a quest of infiltration from London to unearth the earl's perfidy, she is extensively trained and lethal with or *without* weaponry. Do not make the mistake of attempting a tryst with her."

Satisfied with the sudden wariness in the men's gazes as they eyed Heather, Percy barked, "Dismissed!"

The pirates dispersed as the first sprinkling of rainwater fell. But while they might have resumed their tasks, Percy felt their curious scrutiny burning into his rain-splashed skin.

"*Lethal*, Percy?" Heather murmured.

He grunted. "Is that a problem?"

Hell, he couldn't think of another way in which to keep her safe. He trusted her training, knew she was skilled, and yet, like him, she was outnumbered on this ship.

"No," she returned. "Not a problem."

Her gaze grew distant, her bottom lip pulled between her teeth as she worried the tender flesh. *What is she thinking?* Just the knowledge that she was now exposed to a new side of him was decidedly unnerving.

"Are sailors in the habit of collecting fresh rainwater?" she asked abruptly.

He blinked, adjusting to the change in topic. "For many things, yes."

"Might I request a cask be set out to collect rainwater for my plants? They are in dire need of proper care after being so sorely abused in the hold of the *Sapphire*. Many of them perished, and I cannot abide the rest following suit."

Despite himself, a smile tugged at one corner of his mouth. "I shall give it my best."

He stepped closer to whisper in her ear, and a frisson of awareness shot straight to his cock. *Fuck*. Resisting the urge to adjust his falls, he muttered, "We must resume your fighting lessons, Heather. While we are aboard this ship, neither of us is safe."

She audibly swallowed. "Very well."

He pulled back and eyed the sharp blade in her hand. "I'll procure a sheath and holster for you soon.

"Donovan," he called to the man, who had taken to the helm. "Please see Miss Morgan to my cabin."

"Aye, Captain."

Something akin to confusion—*pain?*—flashed in her eyes, and hell if Percy wasn't confused by it. Alarm, and a feeling that he daren't examine too closely, spread across his chest, and before he gave it a moment's thought, he swept forward, cupped her jaw in his hands, and drew her lips to his.

Fuck.

All at once, his skin grew taut and his breath stuttered as need spread like a turbulent wave across his body. He shuddered and angled his head to deepen the kiss. The tip of her tongue touched his, and all his blood flowed downward, making him dizzy with the sudden force of his desire.

Heather lifted on her toes with a soft moan and pressed her free hand to his side. Her skin was hot against his, soft and trembling ever so slightly. Gooseflesh spread over his ribs, extending from beneath her palm, and he desperately wanted to lean into it, to beg her to touch him everywhere. *Hell's tits, what this woman does to me!*

But beneath the tempest of need building within him was the keen awareness of his crew watching them—and of the possible bairn in her womb.

That reminder doused his ardour nigh instantly, and he released her. "Be good. Keep your dirk always at the ready, and I shall see you later."

THE CABIN DOOR closed behind Donovan with a heavy thunk, and despite wanting to venture into the gun deck to learn more about the animals she'd noticed in an enclosure,

Heather turned to observe the spacious accommodations. She blinked. It was obscenely decorated, with nude paintings and statues sporting enormous erections or impossibly hefty breasts.

She snorted a laugh. "Blimey, Butcher."

At a glance, she took in the rest of the room. The furniture was a mixture of styles and themes and screamed confusion—or, perhaps *pirate*, for it seemed obvious that the items had been purloined from different locales.

Atop the shining, checked floor was an enormous burgundy brocade rug and a long dining table surrounded by chairs that filled the centre of the room. On one side of the space stood an aged, white-painted desk and chair, and on the other stood a gilt-flaked chest of drawers topped with a marble washbasin and pitcher.

Against the bay of windows at the rear of the ship was a large bed hung suspended by chains from the ceiling, gently swaying with the movement of the water. Draped above it were red velvet privacy curtains. She made an internal note to ensure the bedclothes were laundered, even while her abdomen quivered with nerves.

Putting a hand to her chest, she leaned back against the cabin's door. She'd just kissed Percy. *Twice.* And she'd had sodding *sex* with the man! A frisson of desire shot through her, and heat gathered low in her belly at the memory of his intimate touches, the snarl on his lips, and the flush of his skin as he came undone. She resisted the urge to clench her thighs together. *Blimey.*

And now she was to share a cabin with him! What would their sleeping arrangement be? Her gaze swung toward the hanging bed, and a flush raced across her chest.

Diversion. Indeed. Diversion was required.

She forced her attention to the ten potted plants placed in

a slapdash manner on the floor near the door, their leaves and petals in varying states of wilt or decay.

"Oh, my darlings," she croaked. "I'm so sorry for what has befallen you."

A sob escaped her throat as she reached for her mother's *Trifolium pratense*, now brown and shrivelled. The dear little red clover grew in many places in England and was easy enough to replace, but this had been her mother's. She picked up the pot, brought it to the window and, ensuring she did not obstruct the path to the bed, set it down.

Doing the same with the other pots, she organized them by size so that the tallest plants did not block the sun's rays from the shortest.

"There you go," she cooed. "Now you all shall have some sunlight."

The ship tilted in a swell, rain splattering the window beside her, and a thought occurred to her. Would her plants not require fastening somehow?

She glanced around the room for inspiration and grinned when she spotted a long length of coiled rope hanging on the wall beside the painting of a nude woman caressing her own breasts. *Thank you, Butcher.*

Using hooks already anchored into the wall beneath the window and along the side wall, Heather secured the plants. Lord, but they needed to be watered. She would need to test the soil as well. How much water would the cask that Percy had set out have collected by now?

Percy...

She sighed as she gave one last tug of the knot and sat back on her heels. There was more to Percy and his life at sea than she'd initially assumed. Of course, she'd known the man had seafaring experience—it was precisely why he'd joined her on assignment—but the reaction of the crew, both pirate and naval alike, was...shocking.

Percy.

Her tryst—her *anonymous* tryst—had been with the very man who'd been training her and her friends in combat for months. How had she not recognized Percy that night? Only half of his face had been obscured, for pity's sake. Even in the darkness, she ought to have recognized him. And his voice...

Now that she thought on it, though, she recalled that they'd spoken only in whispers. Additionally, she'd been distracted by the man's impressive musculature. And his cock.

She snorted at herself, mirth and another healthy wave of arousal sweeping through her.

Percy couldn't be faulted for withholding the secret. Hell, mayhap he'd recognized her from the first. They'd both been eager for the encounter, regardless of their reasons and pretences.

Her fingers toyed absently with the torn hem of her frock, and she grimaced down at it. Browning blood stained the bodice and skirts in both arched and sprayed patterns. Gripping the material in both hands, she tore a length of the material, folded it, then used the clean inside to gently dust the flagging leaves of her plants.

"I wish I had something cleaner with which to dust you," she muttered. "But this dress is ruined, and I haven't my things."

Nor had she anything to wear.

She glanced over her shoulder at Butcher's chest of drawers. "Do you suppose he has anything in my size? Would a 'deadly runner from London' wear the attire of a pirate?"

Her heart gave a little flutter once more at the reminder of Percy's words. They were meant as a warning to the crew, but they'd felt like praise, nonetheless.

Turning from her beloved plants, she made her way to the washbasin and poured a draught of water from the pitcher. She removed her ruined frock and made quick her wash with what appeared to be a clean cloth and some unscented soap situated nearby. She then slid open the bottom drawer in the chest and searched in earnest for something to wear.

The pirate she'd seen had been a rather large man, so it would stand to reason that his attire would be as well. He was, however, in the habit of pilfering his clothes, so there might be something among his things that had yet to be altered to fit his frame.

She ran her fingers over a fine pair of well-worn buckskin breeches. *Soft.* She held them up against her legs and realized with astonishment that they might actually fit. They would be a bit snug in the hips, but they were designed to move and stretch with the body, so they were truly a lucky discovery.

What else would a piratical woman wear? Surely if she was expected to be an experienced runner, she ought to be at ease with taking on a character and fitting in where she mightn't ordinarily. And she *was* an experienced runner, drat it. She would make this work. She would take on the role of "dangerous woman" in order to continue their charade and protect her life.

Now, to complete the *ensemble*.

CHAPTER 12

"I thought we'd thrown all of the dead overboard," Arnold Fitton, the Earl of Hanley, groused, gazing down at the deceased crewmate in distaste.

The man's neck had been broken, and lay twisted at an ungodly angle.

"We *had*, your lordship," replied Sir Rigsby, former officer and new captain of the *Sapphire*. "I don't know what has befallen Grimsby, but he's the second member of the crew to perish since the pirates sailed away."

Arnold shrugged one shoulder, stepped around the fellow, and continued on his way to his cabin. "Mayhap he tripped. The ship rocked rather a lot while the *America* was drawing up next to us." At last their partner ship had reached them, and they were able to begin boarding. He could finally set sail after all of this sodding waiting.

The new captain huffed a breath. "That is unlikely, your lordship. Grimsby, like the rest of the crew, was accustomed to life at sea."

Arnold cut him a sharp sideways glance. "What are you trying to say, man? Spit it out, would you?"

"I'm saying that I believe him to have been murdered."

The earl stopped walking and spun around. Anger flared in his chest at the prospect of another mutiny on board. *What the devil?*

"Additionally," the captain continued, "as the crew was gathering and transferring what few supplies we have left, we could not help but notice that more of our medical supplies have gone missing."

"What?" Arnold grunted. "What do you mean? Have we not accounted for what the crew required after the battle?"

Sir Rigsby nodded. "We did, your lordship. But more has since disappeared. I've questioned the crew and your servants, and we don't know where the items have gone."

"If they were taken by someone among the crew, we'll uncover the truth. We shall search everyone's personal belongings as they're transferred, and the culprit shall be keelhauled."

The captain's eyebrows rose nigh to his hairline. "Keelhauling is an extreme punishment that I could *never* justify, your lordship. And, even if I could, once we're aboard the *America*, the other captain shall be in charge."

Arnold grew still, his gaze boring into Rigsby's until the latter squirmed with unease.

"I shall—just this once—grant you leniency, as this is a new position for you," Arnold said, his voice low and gruff. "But, I assure you, if you read through your predecessor's journal, you will find that per a certain royal's authority, *I* am in command of this vessel." Arnold leaned close, his patience for this man's weakness as a captain entirely gone. "*We shall keelhaul him.*"

With that, he turned and stalked toward his cabin to gather the last of his personal items. He might be older than these young fools, but he was just as ruthless as any man. He was not one to underestimate. No matter what his feckless bride-to-be had done.

The bitch had left him!

The anger that had been simmering in his chest pressed behind his breastbone, threatening to crack his sodding ribs. The heat of his fury spread down his arms and up his neck.

"Your lordship." His valet appeared at his elbow.

"Fuck, where did you come from?"

"My humble apologies, your lordship." The man bowed deeply. "I came to gather your things."

Arnold grunted. "Very well. Get on with it, will you?"

The man scuttled past and filled his arms with Arnold's things, then made to exit. But Arnold halted him when he realized so many pirates had been in the hold.

"Wait," he said, his voice deadly calm despite the fury burning inside him. "Have my chest of boots brought to my cabin on the *America*, will you?"

"Of course, your lordship." The man bowed again, his arms still laden with items, before scurrying out the door.

Arnold had to be certain his documents were safe. He also had to ensure he reached the Americas with a wench on his arm.

Without a woman to wed, Arnold would never be granted his cousin's land and wealth. And the old arse hadn't much time left—which gave Arnold *no* time in which to search for a new betrothed. His course, therefore, was clear. With the additional crew from the *America*, they had to engage bloody Baxter's pirates and take the woman back.

No one embarrassed him. *No one* left him. Indeed. Calluna had made a deal with him. She'd agreed to the arrangement, just as her family had. There was no backing out.

WITH A NOD AT THE PIRATES, who were making repairs along the gun deck and soothing and feeding the fucking animals—of which he was now in charge—Percy closed the cabin door behind him and slumped forward against the cool wood. *Hell*. What was he going to do?

The pressure that had been building in his chest felt nigh on solid, and his skin was flushed, despite the chilled water droplets that raced down his body. He shifted his feet, the gentle sloshing of his boots echoing in the large cabin.

"Good gracious," Heather said from behind him. "You're entirely soaked through!"

He nodded and turned, and his response about the rain all but died in his throat.

"*What...*" he croaked. What the devil was she wearing?

His eyes must have been the size of sodding cannon shot, for the woman was dressed like... Well, like a pirate. She wore buckskin breeches and a billowing white muslin shirt that, due to the lack of a cravat, hung open indecently low to reveal the upper swells of her large breasts, which were lifted by the stays that she'd fastened over the shirt. *Hell's teeth*. How had she managed to fasten it by herself? His gaze was drawn back to the fawn-coloured breeches that hugged her deliciously thick, muscular thighs to perfection, and he salivated. *Salivated*, for Christ's sake. What was bloody well the matter with him?

And she wore no stockings. Her calves and feet were entirely bare as she sat upon a chair and... What the hell was she doing? *Darning stockings?*

"Why have you changed?" he ground out at last. He stepped closer, his feet squelching in his boots.

She looked down at herself and shrugged one shoulder. "My dress was ruined in the battle, and I had naught else to wear. I assumed that a woman of my presumed experience would be comfortable making such concessions."

"I commend your quick thinking—" In an unintentional slip, his gaze dropped to her breasts, and the words stopped.

His throat clicked as he swallowed. "*Jesus*, Heather. Your nipples are visible through the muslin of that shirt. You're veritably nude!"

"Oh, drat." She glanced down at herself once more, then wrapped an arm across her chest to cover the...indecency. "I'd hoped I was wrong. There is a black shirt in the chest of drawers, but I'm afraid it's just large enough that it slips off both of my shoulders. I'd hoped to avoid exposing more skin around the pirates. I'll have to alter it to fit my size."

Her skin was flushed a delicious pink, drawing his gaze up her neck.

"In..." He coughed. "Indeed."

Blood was flowing in a decidedly southern direction, his cock growing heavy with desire and his curst mind filling with thoughts and...*memories.*

Memories of a night that had very likely led to a pregnancy for which he was ill-prepared.

A sudden burst of fear and nerves set his feet into motion, his boots squishing with each step as he paced the width of the cabin. For years he'd not considered his fears of fatherhood particularly noteworthy, for he'd always been so certain that he would never be faced with the circumstance. But—*hell.*

He raked his fingers through his dripping hair.

"Are you well, Percy?"

His head shook before he'd even considered the question. "No."

She stood and came forward, one arm still covering her breasts. "Can I do something? Have they any tea aboard? Shall I fetch you some?"

All at once, a fear leapt from his mouth. "Your stays are too tight."

She frowned. "I beg your pardon?"

"Your stays."

"Yes, I heard you. But I do not believe it is your place to—"

He gestured agitatedly at her abdomen. "You could harm the...the..."

She lifted a brow. "My stomach? While your concerns are noted, they're a bit late. I daresay women across England would have choice words for the creator of the corset and stays—"

"That's not what I meant," Percy interjected.

"Then what?" She huffed a breath. "I acknowledge that I'm a larger woman, Percy. Lacing my stays will always create a bit of a...a *bulge*."

"The *baby*, Heather," he burst out. "Your stays could harm the baby." And fuck if he didn't find all her bulges erotic as hell.

A cough escaped her, and the flush on her cheeks deepened to a fetching crimson. "The *what*?"

The now-familiar unpleasant swirling began in his gut once more. "The *baby*. It has been several weeks since our tryst, and this morning you were nauseated—"

Her loud, abrupt laugh cut him off. "Pardon. But I'm not pregnant, Percy."

Hope fluttered in his chest. "Truly?"

If it were possible, her blush deepened yet further. But she maintained contact with his gaze. "I had my courses aboard the *Sapphire*."

A gusty breath left him in a whoosh, his shoulders sagging as profound relief rushed through him. *There is no baby.*

"Thank fuck," Percy breathed on a laugh, the lightness in his chest making him feel almost giddy. "I cannot tell you just how worried that's made me. Even the thought of it..." He gave a little shiver.

Heather's expression puckered in a frown before it cleared.

"As for our sleeping arrangement," Heather began, then hesitated.

"We've already established a fictional romance between us for the benefit of the crew, but, despite my warnings, I don't trust these men. They are dangerous and accustomed to quick gratification and getting everything they desire. While I trust your skill with a weapon, we cannot risk your being set upon in your sleep an entire deck below me. For that reason, I think it best that you and I share this cabin."

Heather nodded, her arms still crossed over her breasts.

"You shall have the bed. I will sleep elsewhere," he added.

She nodded again, pulling her lips between her teeth to worry them.

With a harsh clearing of his throat, Percy scanned the room and found his satchel leaning against the wide desk. He hurried to it, found a greying black shirt within, and pulled it over his head.

"We need to discuss—"

"No, we don't," she interjected.

He spun to face her. "Pardon?"

She stood, boldly as you please, with her calves and feet bared. "We do not need to discuss that night."

IGNORING the wobble of hurt in her chest, Heather straightened her spine.

Percy spluttered. "But you were a—"

"I am aware of what I was, Percy." Undoubtedly, he'd deduced that he'd taken her virginity. But it did not bear discussing. It was over now. "I made my choice, and I do not regret it."

But, evidently, *he* did. And while she didn't wish for children—with him or *any* man—it bothered her that he found *her* so objectionable.

That thought was lowering, indeed. Her stomach wobbled again, and she gritted her teeth against it.

Despite his obvious distaste for her as a partner in life, it was evident that he found her desirable for bed sport. For, no matter his words, his erection couldn't lie.

And perhaps that was all that she could hope for with this man. Mayhap it would be so with *any* man, and such would be a fine life for her.

Right now, however, she had more pressing matters to which she must attend.

She pressed her lips together before blurting, "Might there be a chamber pot in this cabin? I looked, but I haven't found one."

"Shite," he cursed, his eyes widening. "I'd thought Donovan would have shown you. My apologies. The seat of easement is directly through this door."

He strode to the far-left corner of the cabin, at the end of the wall of windows, where a narrow door seemed to disappear into the wall. He pulled a metal hook, which opened the door to reveal a diminutive wood-planked walkway half-surrounded by green-painted windows. It took two steps for Heather to reach the end, where a bench-like seat featured a hole in it leading directly to the ocean.

Good Lord. What if there's wind—or a storm? Would the seawater not splash her arse? A shiver travelled down her spine at the thought. She'd best move swiftly.

She muttered a thank-you to Percy and ducked inside to perform her necessary functions. By the time she emerged, Percy had donned dry black breeches and boots and had towel-dried his hair.

He sat at the table, surrounded by maps, papers, and implements of which Heather knew nothing. Glancing up at her re-entrance, he gave her a wary smile. Heather's pulse skipped, and she cleared her throat.

"What are you doing?" she asked, striding toward the washbasin to clean her hands.

"I intend to plan our route." He hesitated. "Would you care to join me?"

She gave a silent nod as she returned to the chest of drawers and withdrew the too-large faded black muslin shirt. Retrieving the scissors and sewing implements, she took the proffered seat next to Percy at the table.

It was Percy's turn to clear his throat. "I noticed you'd found a suitable location for your plants."

"Oh, yes. I do hope that rope wasn't important."

He shook his head. "Not at all. I'm pleased you found it useful."

They lapsed into a brief discomfiting silence before Percy broke it. "I instructed Donovan to deliver the bucket of water once it was full. I don't imagine it will be too much longer."

"Thank you." Hope flared at the prospect of reviving her plants. There were so few left...

"We are in a predicament," Percy started, scrubbing at his face then pinching the bridge of his nose. "Pirates are not as common as they once were, due to raids, traps, and a powerful naval presence. Many of the ports pirates once considered a refuge have been overtaken by the navy and are now tokens of warning." His pointed gaze locked on hers. "If we are discovered or—heaven forfend—caught by anyone, we will face the same fate as the men with whom we sail: the noose."

Her throat tightened, but she nodded. She understood the repercussions of being accused of piracy, and she and Percy were by no means prisoners on board this ship. They would certainly go down with the rest of the men, regardless of their innocence.

"Understood. Do you have a plan of where we might go?"

she asked, turning back to her sewing. "We cannot return home aboard a pirate's ship. We would not even make it *near* England's docks in this."

"We must simply find another means of transport."

She lifted a brow. "I would not call that simple, Percy."

"In that you are correct." His lips twisted in a wry smile. "I propose that we sail to a safe port and let the pirates take back their ship. Then, you and I will seek out a frigate that does not fly the Jolly Roger to take us home."

Heather nodded. It seemed a sound enough plan. As much as she hated to consider fault with her leaping so keenly into her assignment, she now ought to reflect on what potential damage being seen at a pirate port might do to her reputation. Upon accepting her mission, she'd anticipated being ruined in the eyes of society, but she'd also expected to return to Bow Street to live and work as a runner and apothecary. But would clients visit a woman who was known to have willingly associated with pirates? Would her disreputable name damage the business?

All at once, a plan began to form like the dawn of a new storm in her mind.

"Once we dock, I should like to use a new name." Surely then her reputation could be saved, if just a little.

A quick frown touched Percy's brow. "A new name? What shall I call you?"

"I shan't change my given name, but I shall take on a married name."

He coughed, his dark skin flushing high on his cheekbones. "Pardon?"

She grinned at him. "It would help my reputation and my appearance if I were to travel as a widow rather than an unmarried woman. What are your thoughts on the name *Mrs. Wood*?"

His lips quirked. "It suits you, I believe."

"Splendid. So, to which port are we sailing?"

Percy bent over the map, his dark hair falling over his forehead as he concentrated. "Truth be told, I'm uncertain where we are." He bit his bottom lip as he opened the notebook and read the last entry, then compared the notes to one of the maps. "The battle was here," he said, pointing. "And we've continued on a westward course, which would take us to approximately *here*."

His finger stopped at a point on the map, and Heather leaned forward to look. They were, of course, in the middle of nothing, a little dot somewhere between large bodies of land.

"It says in Butcher's journal," Percy continued, "that they left Ranter Bay two months ago, and a journey to Madagascar is far greater a distance than continuing on to the Americas."

"Are we not in danger of being caught in the Americas as well? Public hangings of pirates are well-known..."

He nodded. "We are indeed. I know of a port in the south, at San Luis, that is still safe for us. We should reach it in a sennight."

She watched the muscles play under his greying black shirt as he wrote in the journal and plotted the course on the map. Heat built in her belly, and she pressed a hand against the spot in an attempt to quell the inopportune feeling.

"While it's not ideal—due to our time constraints—I daresay it is our best option," she returned, turning her attention back to her sewing.

A sennight on board a pirate ship offered ample opportunity for these bloodthirsty men to try their hands at mutiny... or another sort of attack altogether. A shiver raced down her spine, and in that moment, she reminded herself to keep her dirk always at the ready.

She eyed Percy consideringly. "What might our course of action be should we come across another ship along the journey?"

Percy's lips twisted in thought. "While it will undoubtedly prove a challenge, I'll not have the men murder as Butcher did. They *will* mutiny, however, if I don't permit them to plunder. Devil knows how we would find our way home then." His hands tightened to fists on the table. "Indeed. If we encounter another ship, we *must* engage them."

CHAPTER 13

A loud grumble of complaint pulled Percy from his increasingly wicked musings. He glanced up at Heather as she tied off the thread in her sewing and smiled at her work.

They'd sorted their intentions for their journey, and while he'd written in Butcher's journal, Heather had been sewing her replacement shirt, all while her sodding nipples were visible above her stays. Then she'd gone to work on those ludicrous stockings.

And with every passing moment, he grew more...*heated.* Blast it, this wasn't what he'd intended. He'd not meant for them to be in such close quarters. *But for the next sennight, would it be so wrong to engage in some carnality?*

Heather slid one of the stockings up her calf and tied the ribbon at its top.

Percy forced his gaze away and willed his body to calm.

She hummed, as though in thought, and donned the other stocking, the extra material bunching along the back of her calves. With that, she turned to rummage among Butcher's things, searching a chest and the chest of drawers.

Her newly adjusted shirt billowed with her sudden movement, but it was decidedly more modest than the white had been.

She huffed a breath in exasperation.

"Is something amiss?" he asked, a smirk pulling at his lips.

Placing her hands on her hips, she sighed. "I haven't any boots. I'd hoped to hide my stitching, but I might have to wear my damaged slippers."

Percy stood and came toward her. "I'm certain Butcher must have had a spare pair. If not, there are undoubtedly boots somewhere else on the ship that would fit you."

He joined in her search, peering into several cabinets before settling in front of a large trunk. Heather hummed absently as she moved items in the last cabinet along the wall, and Percy's pulse tripped. It dawned on him, there in the captain's cabin of a pirate ship, that he'd never before experienced a moment like this. He'd been aboard ships and been with women, but *this*... This was decidedly domestic.

This sort of experience was something he'd neither imagined himself having nor thought he desired. And yet, as he knelt before a trunk full of Butcher's shite, his heart told him otherwise.

"Nothing here," Heather murmured, breaking through his thoughts. "You?"

Willing his erratic pulse to calm, Percy cleared his throat and opened the trunk with a loud creak. Sitting on top was a pair of well-worn boots. "As it happens, I've found a pair." He held them out to her. "Try them on?"

With a pleased gasp, she accepted them and sat on one of the table's chairs, bending to put them on. His pulse speeding now, Percy dug deeper among the fascinating items in the trunk.

A large, velvet pouch caught his eye, and he opened it to peer inside. *Fuck*. It was filled with unused condoms. His gut dipped, and his body erupted with nerves and desire, his cock giving one eager throb.

Setting the pouch aside, he continued to dig through the items.

"They're a mite big," Heather announced, stepping toward him. "They'll do for now, but I shall need a replacement soon."

"And so you shall have." Percy nodded, then returned to his search.

"Ah!" he called triumphantly. "I've found what we require!" He turned to Heather with his hand held aloft. "A sheath for your dirk. It mightn't fit perfectly, but it will do for the moment."

With a sodding adorable bounce on her toes and a happy grin, she retrieved her dirk and brought it to him. The sheath appeared to be made for a thin, curved knife, but the length was right. It was a snug fit, but the sheath covered the blade, with the tip poking at the curve in the leather at the bottom.

He retrieved a belt from the trunk and attached the sheath before leaning close to aid Heather in fastening it about her hips—for easy access. But the scent of soap and freshly cleaned skin, and the gentle hitch in her breath, made him freeze. *Hell's tits.*

Tingles raced down his spine, and he suppressed a shiver. There was no doubt that he wanted her again. His body had done little but tell him so every time she was near. But they were on assignment. *Heather's* assignment. And he was there to support her, not seduce her.

Ding-ding, ding-ding... The clang of the dinner bell resonated throughout the ship, breaking the spell holding him in place. He blinked, distancing himself from Heather's decidedly biteable thigh, and closed the trunk.

"What does that mean?" Heather asked.

"It's the dinner bell," he returned, standing. "We can venture down together once you're ready."

Heather's stomach growled. "I'm ready now."

A huffed laugh escaped him at her keenness, but it was followed swiftly by anger. The earl was a right bastard for depriving her of proper sustenance. "Of course." He nodded at her and led the way.

The gun deck had but a few men on duty; they were caring for the animals in the enclosure, restocking and repairing damaged portions of the deck, and cooking in the galley. He and Heather swiftly made their way down the companionway to the mess deck, where the room was warm, humid, and bustling with activity.

Men's voices, and the clank and thump of their eating, sounded around them, and the scent of the sea, sweat, vinegar, salted meat, and the ever-familiar sea biscuits permeated the air. His pulse raced for an entirely different reason, as trepidation clawed up his spine.

Hell. It was the fragrance and the sound of his childhood and youth. A burgeoning panic fizzed in his chest as memories flashed through his mind. Hopelessness, guilt, and fear tore at his throat and squeezed so bloody tight they veritably stole the breath from him.

There wasn't enough air. He could scarcely breathe but for the tightness in his throat. His heartbeat drummed in his ears, thudded against his ribs, and throbbed in his head.

He blinked, his vision wavering, before he forced a slow, deep breath and let it out through pursed lips.

The past must remain in the fucking past, Percy, he reminded himself. He'd found a way out of that life; it didn't have to pull him back in. *It didn't.* This wasn't his childhood.

"Mr. Duncan!" Heather breathed from beside him.

Finally gaining control over his breath and body, Percy

followed her gaze and spotted the bespectacled Scotsman sitting at one of the long tables.

"Come," Percy urged hoarsely. "Let us greet him."

She nodded. "Yes, please. I would very much like to continue our discussion on the apothecary and what medicinal plants I would be best suited to grow."

He started forward, noting with irritation the curious and admiring gazes of the other pirates as they passed. *This isn't permanent.* He closed his eyes briefly, then pasted a half smile on his lips as they approached the surgeon.

I can leave when I want, his mind screamed at his rapid pulse and the alarming tingling sensation rippling down his arms to his fingertips. *I am in control of my time on this ship.*

DESPITE THE OVERWHELMING aroma of vinegar, Heather's mouth watered at the plate of food Percy placed on the table before her. There were strips of dried, dark, and seasoned meat, a steaming pile of lentils, stalks of pickled carrots and asparagus, and what appeared to be a large oblong bun. After weeks of having her food monitored so closely by the earl—and before that, by her aunt and uncle—she was not only famished but desirous to savour every bite of her freedom.

Percy sat beside her as Duncan continued talking.

"Rosemary, ginger, an' fennel are invaluable," the surgeon said, listing the items on his fingers. "An' ye cannae go wrong with comfrey, bistort, an' goat's rue. I ken ye 'ave some o' them wot I listed, but 'ave they survived?"

Heather nodded along, eagerly soaking in the information as she swallowed her first bite of the bewilderingly sweet lentils. "They require water and sun. I believe that most will survive once properly cared for." She leaned closer, excitement squirming in her belly. "Now, what *part* of each plant need I dry to best aid an apothecary?"

She was exceedingly aware of Percy's rapt perusal of her face as she conversed with Duncan. The desire to question him was on the tip of her tongue, but she was suitably diverted by her delicious meal and the surgeon's knowledge.

Duncan's eyes lit up. "There are several methods o' preparation tha' I can show ye, but plants such as chickweed—or *Stellaria media*—have leaves tha' are useful fresh in a poultice. There are salves, teas, an' liniments tha' require dryin' the leaves, flowers, or buds, but mayhap I can show ye instead?"

"Oh, that would be lovely! I brought a journal with me in which to document all I learn. Might I meet with you on the morrow to discuss this further?" Her pulse fluttered with anticipation and eagerness. She was already looking forward to filling her mother's journal with everything new that she'd learned.

"I'd be 'appy t' 'elp." Duncan's eyes creased in the corners as he smiled and stood. "Come t' the surgeon's rooms when ye like."

And, with a tug on his forelock, he departed.

With excitement bubbling through her and a grin on her lips, Heather lifted a piece of dried meat and took a bite. Her jaw worked to break through it, while the salty spices burst on her tongue.

"Mmm," she hummed, glancing at Percy. She swallowed the bite and grinned. "This is quite good. It feels rather liberating to eat what I desire." *And to wear what I desire*. These feelings were entirely new and thrilling. It was akin to what she'd felt when she'd begun working for Bow Street.

"It is. You are welcome to eat as much as you please. There is plenty." His dark eyes glimmered with something that Heather couldn't quite decipher, then he jutted his chin toward her plate. "The pickled vegetables are often intriguing.

Some have spice that tingles on the tongue. When that happens, the sea biscuit is excellent at cooling the heat."

"Sea biscuit?" Heather puzzled.

Percy nodded, swallowing another bite of his food. "It is made of water, flour, and salt. They're simple, but they cleanse the palate and help fill your stomach."

A muscle twitched in his jaw, and she suspected that there was something about the food that bothered him. Mayhap he'd eaten so many that he'd grown tired of the flavour. But... his entire demeanour had grown rigid, his spine stiff and muscles taut. Something was bothering him.

"Are you—" she began, but the ship pitched sideways, slamming her into his side.

"It's the storm," he said, as the ship's bell began to ring.

Men rose from their seats as Percy shoved food into his mouth. Then he rose as well and urged her to her feet.

He clasped her arm and gazed unwaveringly into her eyes. "Bring your plate to the cabin. Stay low, stay safe. I will return at the end of my shift."

She gave a short nod, clasping her plate close. "You stay safe as well."

His lips tightened, and he leaned in to press his mouth to her ear. "Remember, Heather: you are fearsome and formidable."

And with that, he was gone, up the companionway, leaving her standing there with her plate in her hand and warmth buzzing through her abdomen. *Fearsome and formidable.*

The ship swayed, forcing Heather to catch her footing. *Best get moving.* She hurried for the companionway on unsteady feet, when a voice halted her.

"Y' don't look so dangerous. Does she, men?" The voice was gruff, and it skittered up her spine with a thread of alarm.

"Naw, she don't," another voice said.

"I bet she's soft, an easy frig," said a third.

Fearsome, Heather reminded herself, despite the nerves tingling up and down her legs. She needed to prove her mettle to these men.

She turned to face them and noted with a pang of anger that she recognized one of them as a crewmate from the *Sapphire*. *The cur.*

One man stepped closer, his smile one full of menace and his eyes half-lidded with desire.

Fear seized her, and all at once every bit of her training vacated her mind. *Blast.* Surely there was *something* left that might prove useful? A strike? A block? *Christ*, what was the best method in which to break a man's nose?

She stepped back from the approaching man, and the sheath bumped against her hip. *Of course. My dirk.*

With one hand on her plate, she clasped and brandished her dirk with the other. "Back away."

One of the men's eyebrows lifted with what appeared to be admiration, while the other pirate and the previous *Sapphire* crew member simply looked increasingly pleased as they continued their advance.

Oh, Lord. I might actually have to use *this!*

"Look, men, she 'as a little blade," the advancing pirate said.

"Indeed," she said, marvelling at the calm in her voice. "And I shall gut you with it if you come any closer." She entered what she knew to be the *en garde* position in fencing and prepared herself for what might come next. *Please let me remember something useful.*

The first man reached out to clasp her wrist, and she instinctively slashed the dirk through the air, slicing into the blackguard's hand.

He pulled back with a shout as the ship pitched sideways. The desire in his gaze turned swiftly into malevolence, and his hands clenched into fists, no doubt to stem the flow of blood.

Heather caught her footing and readied herself once more.

"Get her, men," he growled. "I want this bitch taken down."

Her stomach twisted, but she kept her stance.

The other pirate approached tentatively from the front, while the sailor from the *Sapphire* rounded behind her. *Blast.*

Work fast and get out.

The sailor attacked first, his arms coming around her waist and knocking her off balance. Some of her lentils slipped from her plate, and hot fury raced through her. *My food!* She would *not* let these men dictate her time on the *Pandora*. She was in charge, and she was dratted hungry.

With a flourish, she spun the dirk in her palm and thrust the blade between the sailor's ribs. His hoarse scream rang in her ears, but she hadn't the time to think as he released her. She pulled the dirk out and brandished it at the pirates before her.

"I shan't warn you again," she said low, grateful that the sudden trembling she felt didn't reflect in her voice.

The pirates, at last, retreated, and she backed to the companionway.

"That's enough, men," another pirate—*blimey*, it was Stubbs!—called over the din of the bell. "You 'eard th' cap'n. Get t' yer stations."

He was a bit late, but she appreciated the show of support nonetheless.

Oh Lord, Heather! Did you just kill a man? She chanced a glance, and a wave of profound relief swept over her. The sailor held a hand to his side as he cursed her name, but he was alive. And it appeared that he wasn't bleeding too badly. He would survive.

"Thank you," she called after Stubbs as she sheathed her dirk.

Stubbs tugged on his forelock before hurrying to his duties.

Still clutching awkwardly at her plate, Heather clumsily made her way up the companionway onto the gun deck, where men were scrambling to ensure that items were fastened down and the animals were safe. Her heart was all but entirely in her throat, and her skin hummed with trepidation. Would any of *these* pirates attempt an assignation with her? She swallowed her fear, determined to ignore them, and darted into the safety of the captain's cabin, closing the door behind her.

CHAPTER 14

"*Another swell*!" Percy shouted, rainwater spraying from his lips.

He widened his stance slightly to accommodate the movement as the *Pandora* tilted bowsprit-first into the approaching wave. His grip tightened on the helm's handles, slippery though they were with rainwater and the ocean's spray.

"Direction?" he asked his second helmsman nearby.

The man gazed into one of the compasses set into the binnacle and shouted, "Five degrees west-southwest, Captain!"

A wave crashed against the side of the ship, spraying water through the air. The ship groaned, and Percy cursed. They'd been tossed about in this storm for hours. Now he and his pirates were battling against each wave deep into the darkness of night.

Another swell appeared before them, and he spun the wheel toward it.

"*Brace yourselves*!" he hollered.

Up they went, tilting toward the dark clouds pouring water down on them. They crested the wave, and Percy braced as the *Pandora* tipped down. *Bwoosh!* They landed hard, the spray reaching across the planks of the quarterdeck before being sucked back into the ocean.

Wave after wave tossed them about like a leaf upon a river, all while Percy fought to keep the *Pandora* upright.

A smaller swell tipped them forward, and he once more tightened his grip on the helm as seawater crashed over them. The next was yet smaller. Gradually, the whipping wind died down, and with it, the tempestuous waves. The rain didn't abate, nor did the sky clear, but at last the ship settled into a gentle, steady rocking.

He stood thusly for long moments, braced for the storm potentially gathering strength once more. But, as time passed, the waves continued to gentle.

Percy loosened his grip on the helm's handles and adjusted his stance, his muscles aching with tension. "Direction?" he called to the second helmsman.

The shorter man wiped back his dark locks and examined the compass. "Five degrees north-northeast, Captain."

Percy cursed and turned the wheel, trying to get them back on course.

A crate wobbled with the turn, its movement catching Percy's attention not for the first time that evening, and his mind once again strayed to Heather. Christ, but he hoped that she'd weathered the storm well enough. Her cask of water would do her plants little good, however, if it was full of salt from the ocean.

"You, there!" he called to one of the pirates, ensuring the cannons remained secured. "Empty that cask and refasten it to the bulwark."

"Aye, Captain." The man tugged on his forelock and hurried to do as he was bid.

Despite himself, Percy warmed at the thought of Heather's joy at having the water to feed her beloved plants. It bewildered him, his reaction to her. He desired her, of course, but this...*attachment* he felt for her was veritable tosh. Nothing could come of it, and he knew that, damn it.

While he would grant that the women of Bow Street were unlike others of the *haut ton*, Heather was still a lady. For all he knew, she might well desire children—which he would *never* wish to provide. She was above his station—which was entirely unavoidable, as he was the bastard son of a pirate—and...sod it, she deserved better than him. He had no intention of saddling any woman with the burden of his name, and he most certainly had no desire to do so to a woman that he actually—

He cursed. *Why, damn it?* He was so sodding attracted to the woman, with her melodious voice, sunny hair and disposition, and fiery determination. Hell, but she was braver than most men he knew. And every bit of her, every new facet of her personality that he discovered, all tugged at him, drawing him closer to her when he damned well ought to leave her to her assignment.

Shaking himself, he called to his second helmsman, "Direction?"

"Southwest."

Percy stayed the wheel and barked orders at the crew, while Donovan appeared beside him.

"Shift change, Captain," he said.

Percy nodded. "Report?"

"One man injured—fell getting out of his hammock and landed on the table—and three seasick. One member of the crew from the *Sapphire* was stabbed and bears a blade wound. No complaints from your woman."

My woman.

"Wait." Percy frowned. "Someone was stabbed?"

Donovan nodded. "He and others approached your woman with lewd intentions. I'm told she defended herself admirably."

Hot fury shot through Percy's veins, and he bit back a dark curse. "Noted. We are travelling to San Luis and are currently directed southwest."

The man's eyes lit at the mention of the pirate port—and the prospect of drink, gambling, and women.

"Aye, Captain!" he replied enthusiastically, taking the helm.

Percy bid the man good night and, with a wave, withdrew down the companionway and slipped into his dark cabin.

AT LAST, the storm had eased, and Heather was able to curl herself between the bedclothes, her mother's journal clutched tightly to her chest as the ship gently rocked and rain splattered the wall of windows. Exhaustion pulled at her, but her mind wouldn't quiet enough for her to slip into sleep. She was grateful, though, that her seasickness hadn't returned.

Compassion filled her at the sound of the animals' distress. There hadn't been animals on the *Sapphire*, but it made sense why they would bring them aboard, particularly for long journeys.

She sighed.

She'd spent the majority of the storm saving her plants from tipping over, guarding her mother's journal—and, within it, the earl's documents—or clinging to the bed as it swung wildly back and forth. But so much had happened in just one day, it was as though her brain was determined to analyse every action she'd taken.

A tremor of trepidation and revulsion shook her from head to foot as she recalled the encounter on the mess deck... and the battle of that morn. She'd intentionally injured those men. And she would do so again. The shock of that truth rippled through her every time it crossed her mind. Yes, she'd been trained in such combat, but she'd not truly considered what that might *mean*.

The cabin's door slid open on silent hinges, and Heather pulled her dirk from its sheath and held it at the ready, poised to attack. It was only when she heard a thump and Percy's muted curse that she relaxed and put the weapon away. She'd intended to lock the door, but didn't know if Percy would be able to enter if she fell asleep.

His boots sloshed, and his clothes made wet slapping sounds as he moved about the space. He cursed softly again, and a smile quirked her lips, the awful wobble in her abdomen being gradually replaced by the warmth of familiarity and affection.

Snick.

"Fuck," he muttered.

Snick.

"Fuck," he repeated.

Heather's chest seized, all pleasant feelings fleeing at once. *Fire.* With her heart and mind still veritably besieged with worry and fear, she could not countenance yet another added atop it.

"No," she breathed, sitting up abruptly.

"Hell's tits, Heather!"

His dark, shadowy figure stood frozen near the chest of drawers, dim moonlight glinting off the glass enclosure of the lantern he'd been attempting to light.

"No fire," she repeated, her voice quavering. "Please."

"Very well." He set something aside—no doubt the flint and steel—and withdrew an item from his satchel.

"How do you fare?" she asked.

He huffed a breath. "Sore. And wet. You? Any seasickness?"

"No. Merely tired."

He grunted in return, then pulled his drenched shirt over his head.

Heather's core gave a throb as instant desire swelled, and her heart hiccoughed.

Privacy, Heather's mind whispered. The man required it. But her gaze would not be deterred. Instead, it was transfixed on the movements of his dark figure: carefully removing his sodden clothing, scrubbing his body dry with a towel, and donning a pair of breeches. And there she sat, boldly eying him through the dim, hazy light from the window at her back. And he let her.

Her pulse sped, and she fought to keep her breathing steady.

He padded several steps toward the bed before he hesitated, the broad expanse of his chest rising and falling rapidly. He was, no doubt, deliberating on where he might sleep. Heather's stomach dipped.

If they shared the bed, their proximity might encourage touching...might lead to sex. Her core throbbed with want at the thought, and she swallowed convulsively. *Hell*, but her body was flooded with desire. She'd been intimate with the man before, and her maidenhead was gone. What would additional trysts with the man do apart from bring pleasure and delight?

She would ensure that they took precautions—whatever that entailed—and she would enjoy every moment that she could with Percy while she had him. *If* he wished to, of course.

Her heart hiccoughed, and her pulse sped yet further, no doubt flushing her skin.

And, without hesitation, she flicked up the bedclothes beside her, offering a silent invitation.

"Are you certain?" he asked, his voice rough, likely from hours of bellowing orders through the storm.

"Yes." She lay back against her pillow and patted the space

next to her at his continued hesitation. "Come along, then. You needn't touch me if that makes you uncomfortable. But you require rest, Percy."

He moved, then, the bed swaying and dipping with his weight as he joined her. The dim light was better nearer the window, and she drank him in. His skin was half in shadows and half coated in the milky blue light of the storm, the raindrops sliding on the glass panes creating a pattern upon his skin. His tattoos were only inky splotches in the obscurity. She turned on her side to face him, not bothering to hide her perusal as he settled himself.

"It doesn't," he murmured.

"Mmm?" she hummed in question.

"Touching you," he clarified. "It doesn't make me uncomfortable."

"Oh."

His dark eyes glistened as he scanned her face. "It...*you* arouse me, Heather. And I don't wish to make you feel—"

"You arouse me, as well," she whispered, cutting off his words. More heat flooded her, spreading quivering desire through her core.

The click of his throat as he swallowed was loud to her ears. His gaze was intense, his breath coming quickly. And boldness took root.

Sliding forward, she pressed her lips to his. His grunt of shock turned into a moan as he deepened the kiss. *Yes.* Heart fluttering, she matched his fervour. She knew what she wanted, and she no longer wished to deny herself, if Percy was willing.

With another nervous flutter in her belly, Heather clasped his hand in both of hers and guided him brazenly toward her cleft.

"*My god,* Heather," he groaned. "You're nude!"

She shrugged one shoulder. "I'm wearing a shirt. It was so large I thought to wear it as a night-rail."

He groaned again, and she guided his fingers until they dipped inside her. She gasped and widened her legs to give him more room.

"*Fuck*, Heather, you're already so wet for me." He shifted closer.

"It—" She gasped again, and her voice hitched as his devilish fingers explored. "It happens all the...time."

His voice grew hoarse. "Does it?"

She nodded, her hair rubbing against the pillow. "Nearly every time...I look at...you."

"*Fuck*."

Then his lips were on hers once more, his tongue delving hungrily while his fingers slipped out of her to circle her cleft. A moan escaped her, and shocks of pleasure tingled down her centre.

But she wanted more. She wanted *him*, his body, his cock inside her, bringing her to the climax that she knew would come. So she touched him.

His skin was hot as she trailed her hands down his muscled abdomen.

"I want you," she breathed, unfastening his breeches.

He hissed a breath between clenched teeth. "*Yes*. Touch me there," he urged. "Take me in your hands."

His breeches gaped, and he sprang free, heavy, hard, and leaking. Heather eagerly clasped him in a tight grip and slid her hand up his length, marvelling in the smoothness of his skin there.

He moaned.

"Do you like that?" she asked, her voice husky and entirely foreign to her ears.

"*Yes*. My god, *yes*." His fingers, which had stilled while she worked, began thrusting inside her again, pulling another moan from her lips.

More!

Feeling even bolder, she slid her hand alongside his, dipping and coating her fingers with her dew.

"What—"

Then, she clasped him, covering his cock and sliding her hand easily along his shaft.

"*Oh, fuck,*" he grunted, his own fingers continuing their delicious swirl of her cleft and winding her nerves tight. "Heather, I can't... I want to..."

He lifted up over her and tugged himself free of his breeches, cursing when they got caught on his heel, then helped her off with her shirt.

"I need to be inside you. But first..." He leaned over the swaying bed and reached for something on the floor. He returned with an odd-looking sheath with a ribbon.

"What is that?" she asked.

He carefully slid the thin coating over his erection, stretching whatever it was tight before tying off the ribbon at the base. "It's a condom. Made to prevent pregnancy."

She blinked. "That's rather brilliant. With what is it made? And where did you get it?"

He huffed a breathy laugh. "I'll tell you and your curious mind later. Right now, I need you to come."

Positioning himself between her thighs, he bent to lick a path up one inner thigh. Her breath hitched, her hips tilting upward of their own accord. She knew what he was about to do, and she could scarcely wait. Nerves buzzed and tingled throughout her body, and more molten heat flooded the apex of her thighs.

"My god, look at you," he breathed.

She resisted the urge to squirm under his perusal, but the

truth was that she wanted this, wanted him to stare his fill and be aroused by her, just as she was by him.

Then he lay himself upon his elbows, wrapped his arms around her thighs, and licked a stripe from her arse to her cleft. A cry was wrenched from her throat, and her back arched. Percy chuckled, his breath hot against her, as he tightened his grip on her hips.

"I'm going to fuck you with my tongue until you come," he breathed against her. "Then I'm going to take this sweet little cunny and pound out my pleasure."

Her eyes slid closed at his words. "Oh my god, yes!"

He licked her again, first dipping into her core and then swirling his tongue around her cleft. Her hips rolled, and her inner muscles clenched.

"More, Percy," she begged. "Please, *more*."

He grunted and complied. Shifting his weight to one elbow, he slid two thick fingers into her passage while creating gentle suction on her cleft.

She panted, and he curled his fingers, finding a spot inside her that sent sharp bolts of pleasure racing up her spine. His tongue swirled again, and then he sucked, then swirled and sucked...

Her legs began to shake, her head growing dizzy from the onslaught of pleasure, until at last she burst. Head spinning and back arching, a scream of "*Percy*!" filled the air.

He continued his ministrations while she came down from her climax, then he withdrew his hand and used her wetness to coat his sheathed cock.

"My turn," he growled, lifting up over her.

Gripping himself, he guided his cock into her and thrust, filling her in one swift movement. She gasped, and he groaned. Then he started to move. With a few rapid snaps of his hips, he had her desire heightened once more. She clasped at his shoulders. The sound of their slapping flesh, rapid breathing, and steady moans was lewd and erotic, and it only served to enhance her enjoyment.

"I want—" he growled, his lips curling back to show a flash of his teeth in the darkness.

She panted. "What...do you...want?"

"I want more...of you." His dark gaze locked onto hers as his hips continued to pump. "I want to fuck you against the wall...on the desk... I want to...take you from behind... To... claim your body, and mark it...with my teeth." His head tilted back on a throaty moan.

A series of thrills went up her spine, and her eyes nearly rolled backward, but she made sure to catch his gaze again. She'd heard of such things from her friends but had never imagined she'd experience them. But with Percy... *Yes. Hell, yes.* "I want that too."

*F*uck. Percy's ballocks drew up tighter against him and threatened to spill at her words. But he wouldn't let them. Not yet. He wasn't done making her come.

Without another word, he wrapped his arms tightly around her and lifted. She squeaked, and her sweet cunny tightened around his cock, pulling another groan from his throat. Bloody hell, this woman would be the death of him.

He waited for the bed to swing back down before he placed his foot on the rug and stood with Heather clinging to him, his cock still deep inside her. As much as he wanted to try out every position he'd fantasized about, he knew he wouldn't last. The woman had come so prettily, and she tasted like fucking heaven.

In two long strides, he pressed her up against the wall of windows. She gasped, no doubt at the cold, and he quickly dipped to suck one of her nipples into his mouth.

Her gasp turned into a moan, and he smiled against her, rolling the little bud gently between his teeth before releasing her with a pop.

"*Percy.*"

He kissed his name from her lips, sucking her tongue into his mouth as he resumed his thrusting. Tingles shot down his spine, warning him that his climax was imminent. But he wanted her to come again, to come *with* him. So he pressed her harder against the glass, using his weight to keep her up as he let his hands wander.

One hand slid between them to tease her little pleasure spot, swirling and flicking, while his other slid around her arse to tease her hole.

She gasped against his lips. "*Percy*!"

"Will you let me, sweetheart? Will you adventure with me?"

Her eyes were wide as he circled her hole and her cleft simultaneously with his fingertips while thrusting his cock in her.

"Oh my god. Oh, Percy, that's—"

Her chest rose and fell with each breath, and her mouth dropped open in bliss as he fucked her.

"Come for me," he urged, increasing his ministrations.

"I..." she gasped.

Her cunny squeezed him tight just before her head fell back against the glass, her nails digging into the flesh of his shoulders and neck. And, at last, he broke. His ballocks drew up tight as he thrust one last time, emptying himself into the condom as shudders wracked his frame.

They stood thusly for several long minutes, their breathing gradually returning to normal, before Percy lowered Heather to her feet.

"Are you well?" he asked, twining a lock of her fallen hair behind her ear.

She shuddered in his arms. "Very well, indeed."

He grinned and pressed a kiss to her temple. "Come, let us get clean and get some rest."

THE GLASS of brandy slid across the table as the *America* tilted, and Arnold Fitton, the Earl of Hanley, caught it before it knocked into the table's short rail. They ought to do something about the dreadful to and fro of the ship. It had grown tiresome.

"It would appear that they've continued on to the Americas," the captain was saying.

Arnold's ears perked, his fury barely banked beneath the surface of his skin. "Are you certain?"

"The ship's original direction—"

"Never mind that," Arnold interrupted, impatience riding him. "Do you know *where* in the Americas they aim to dock?"

The captain's lips tightened. "There is a place in the *Golfo Mexicano* where our warships have found success finding pirates, but no raid has yet taken place. There is a good chance that the *Pandora* has gone—"

"Then we shall follow," Arnold interjected again. "I must have my bride returned."

Indeed. She'd stolen something of great value to him, and he needed it back. He also needed the bitch to suffer.

The captain inclined his head. "As you've mentioned before, your lordship. We are doing all we can, and while our *America* is a fast ship, the *Pandora* had several—"

"I care not!" Arnold slammed his fist on the table, rattling the tableware and halting all other conversation in the wardroom. "They were no doubt slowed by repairs after the battle. But *we* are on a fresh vessel. We *will* find their ship—whether it's moored, sailing, or sunken. And we *will* retrieve my intended from those *goddamned pirates*!"

Pressure swelled in his cheeks and neck, as it always did when rage consumed him. But he continued to stare the fools down.

The captain of the *America*—whose name Arnold couldn't be bothered to remember—inclined his head. "Of course, your lordship." He turned to one of his officers. "Inform the navigation officer and helmsman that we shall chart a course for the *Golfo Mexicano*."

Arnold's heart leapt in anticipation.

"Right away, Captain." The officer slid his chair back and saluted before darting from the wardroom.

"There is much to be considered, of course, if we are to venture into pirate territory." The captain dipped a fresh roll into the sauce on his plate, then took a large bite.

"Naturally," Arnold drawled, an eyebrow lifted in challenge. "But we shall ready ourselves."

"I've been informed," said one of the officers, "that more rations have gone missing. I believe it's time we address the crew…"

Arnold tuned him out, irritation swiftly clouding his anticipation. He *would* search this *Golfo Mexicano* for Calluna. She would not be free of him so easily. And then, naturally, he would marry the wench, with his aged fool of a cousin as witness, procure the entailment, kill the bastard, and get his wife good and pregnant with his heir.

A SENNIGHT later

"EXCELLENT," Percy said encouragingly. "Now strike your blows."

With practised movements, Heather aimed at his nose, his groin, and his eyes, all of which Percy blocked in quick succession.

"Well done." He grinned at her.

Her eyes lit with determination. "Again."

He nodded. "I shall attack. You block me."

To his chagrin, his body flared to life each time they made contact. And each time she clasped his wrist or brushed his hand, his pulse sped further. And not from the exertion.

He made for another attack, reaching for her throat with both hands, when she lifted her arms between his and spread them wide. *Sodding hell*, did it arouse him. She was learning so much, improving with every passing day.

"*Yes*," he cheered. "That's precisely how it's done!"

She beamed at him, and his chest squeezed. The past sennight had been a veritable whirlwind of activity between them. During the day, he manned the helm, and she tended to her plants and learned from Duncan. Then they would spar, and Heather would teach him all she'd learned. And in the evenings, they would fuck. It was amazing. *She* was amazing.

Aiming for a surprise attack, Percy gripped her elbow and pulled. Pride swelled in his chest as she spun, withdrew her sheathed dirk, and pressed it beneath his chin.

He chuckled, but his laughter swiftly fled as she pressed herself against him. Lust hummed through his body, and he groaned.

"Don't tempt me, woman, unless you wish to be bent over the chest of drawers and taken from behind."

Heat flared in her green eyes, and she tossed the dirk aside, fully crushing herself against his chest. "You cannot threaten something as delicious as that and not deliver, sir."

His heart hiccoughed, and he turned them, using his size and experience to take control and press her arse against the chest of drawers.

"Is that what you want right now, Heather?" he growled. "For me to be rough when I take you?"

A low moan escaped her, and he took that as confirmation. He knew what she wanted, and, by damn, he would give it to her.

He gripped her hips and spun her, then ground the ridge of his erection into her arse. She gasped, and he exulted. Reaching around her, he made quick work of the falls of her breeches and tugged, exposing the perfect globes of her arse to his view.

"Put your elbows on the chest of drawers," he ground out.

Her breath hitched as she bent forward.

"That's right. Oh, you're so good. *Fuck*, and so wet for me already."

His gaze trailed down her exposed form, his cock straining to be released at the sight of her glistening cunny. He wanted to lick her, to spend his time worshipping her body. But she wanted hard and fast, and he would bloody give it to her.

Gripping a cheek in each of his hands, he squeezed them simultaneously. Little tremors of pleasure danced along his nerves and quivered in his abdomen. He loved how the flesh of her arse bulged between his fingers. *Hell's tits*, but he wanted to bite her.

"Stay just like that," he instructed, his voice rough. "Do not move."

Condoms, he reminded himself. Must have those. Another element might be fun for her, as well. He hurried to the bed to retrieve a condom, then in two strides he reached behind the chest to withdraw a mirror. He placed it on the chest of drawers in front of Heather, leaning it against the wall.

"Hold this steady," he told her.

She did, clasping the bottom edges as she locked gazes with him through the reflection.

"Now," he grunted. "Keep your gaze on me. Watch me fuck you."

Her neck was flushed, and her eyes were half-lidded, but she nodded.

His trembling fingers fumbled with the buttons at his falls, and he muttered a short curse before he finally slid the material down his legs. His cock was painfully rigid and jumped at each touch of his hands as he donned the condom and tied off the ribbon.

The grin of triumph on his lips was fleeting as he stepped forward, gripped himself, and wet the tip of his cock with her dew. He hissed.

"Please, Percy," she whimpered.

"Are you ready for me?" he asked, poised at her entrance.

She spread her legs further and tilted her hips upward, presenting herself beautifully for him.

Fuck.

"*Yes*, Percy," she moaned. "Take me, touch me. *Anything.* Please."

Hell, that gift of *carte blanche* both swelled his chest and tightened his cods. And he wasted not one second more, thrusting into her tight, slick cunny until he was fully inside. He gripped her hips, holding her hard against him.

A keening moan tore from her lips, and her eyes slid closed.

"Eyes on me," he grunted, sliding out and in again.

She met his gaze, her green eyes ablaze with lust. "My god, Percy, this angle. You're reaching new places..." Her words trailed off on a gasp as he snapped his hips in a thrust.

He couldn't go easy, couldn't take his time. His body was afire, and he needed more.

SHUDDERS ROCKED through Heather's frame as Percy thrust into her. His eyes were dark and heavy with want, and his big hands gripped her hips. It was heady, indeed, being the object of his desire. And he was the object of hers. There was something tangibly exciting about watching him this way, his skin flushed and slicked with sweat as his hips snapped and his cock hit all of the spots that thrilled her deep inside.

Pleasure built inside her, but she knew that without touching her *pearl*—as Percy had once called it—she would never find release. Her hand twitched on the mirror, her desperation showing in her gaze.

"Please, Percy," she begged. "I need to—" She broke off on a moan as he slammed into her.

He gave her a half grin. "I know what you need, sweetheart."

Releasing one of her hips, he reached around her until he found her slickened pearl and gave it a flick.

A cry of pleasure was pulled from her throat, and her legs began to tremble.

"Keep your eyes on me," he urged, swirling his fingers in steady, delicious circles.

He continued to thrust. Their panting breaths and the lewd slapping and suction of their joining filled the air around them. It was too much. It was so fast.

Her climax came upon her suddenly, the tingling rushing up her legs without warning before bursting like fireworks of pleasure in her blood and wrenching a scream from her throat.

And all the while, she kept Percy's gaze.

"*Fuck*," he ground out, the pink in his cheeks deepening as his rhythm faltered. "Fuck. *Fuck*."

With a hoarse growl, he tightened his grip on her hips and stilled deep inside her, his cock pulsing as he released his seed into the condom.

"With salves, it is crucial tha' ye correctly prepare th' herbal oil an' allow it t' infuse fully," Duncan instructed, his gaze intent on Heather. "Donnae think ye can skip a step, or th' salve willnae be potent, an' ye risk swelling, the fever, an' amputation. De ye ken?"

Heather nodded, jotting the note in her mother's journal, then looked back up at the older sailor. He'd quickly become a friend. His flushed red cheeks and bushy beard were familiar now and brought her comfort among the ever-present threats aboard the *Pandora*.

"Now, let's see." He turned toward the crates of ingredients and hovered over them.

This surgeon's room was much like the one aboard the *Sapphire*, though the racks were filled with the previous surgeon's items while Duncan's filled crates lined the floor along the wall nearest the examination table. He'd cleared the desk of parchment and notebooks and placed the stacks of books upon additional shelves behind the chair in which Heather now sat. Heaven knows how the previous surgeon had worked in such clutter, but he was not around to ask. As much as she didn't care to think on it, Heather suspected that he'd perished during the battle with the *Sapphire*.

She cleared her throat and shook her thoughts clear, ready once more to learn. "Might I use one of the herbal oils that we created this week to make a salve?"

"Aye. First, I'll tell ye how t' make it, an' then if ye decide t' use one, ye can." He tapped the side of the crate as he inspected the bottles within. "Ye mustn't rush into it, ye ken. Ye must carefully consider if th' oil will serve any purpose as a salve. Yer calendula oil mixture, fer example, is good t' pour over wounds, an', depending on 'ow severe, ye might wish t' rub it in as a salve. 'Tis ideal t' 'ave both on 'and, aye?" He withdrew a jar with a flourish. "Aha! Th' beeswax. Blasted thing was hiding."

She grinned at him before dipping her pen in ink and jotting the information down.

The next hours passed companionably, with Duncan first instructing her and then guiding her in the making of salves. She'd already learned a vast amount about apothecaryship—in theory, at least—and could scarcely await her return to England to put her newfound knowledge to work.

But what would that mean for her relationship with Percy?

Her thoughts elsewhere, she bid an absent farewell to Duncan before leaving the aft platform and ascending the companionway to the mess deck.

The last sennight had passed in a flurry of activity, and she didn't wish for it to end. She knew about their plans to reach San Luis and search for another vessel to bring them home, but Percy would no longer be captain, and their time alone together would be at an end. And, while it didn't have the comforts of home, she'd come to adore their cabin with a swinging bed.

It was difficult to fathom that mere weeks ago, she'd been a spinster wallflower sneaking past her aunt and uncle's watchful eyes to carry out assignments with her friends on Bow Street. And now she was, for all intents and purposes, a pirate. *Not only a pirate*, her inner voice amended. She was a pirate having nightly—sometimes daily *and* nightly—sex with a pirate captain.

As exhilarating as it had been, being with Percy for the past sennight, a part of her grew apprehensive about what the future might hold. What would happen to them once they *did* reach home?

The earl would be publicly humiliated, tried, and hung for treason, leaving her his ruined former intended who had journeyed for weeks, without a chaperone, on board ships of men. She would move into the rooms above the Bow Street offices as planned, continue to take on assignments, and create an apothecary for the women there.

But Percy... Did he wish to continue their dalliance? It was entirely possible that he considered their trysts just that: convenient relief of their desires while living in close quarters. And while *she* might wish to continue their assignations once they returned home, she would not force the man into something he didn't want.

The bubbling of nerves in her abdomen intensified, and her chest squeezed at the thought.

She took the last step from the companionway to the gun deck, and faltered. Three familiar men stood before her, their gazes blazing with both hatred and desire. It was the men who'd attempted an attack on her a sennight prior.

"Look 'oo it is, boys," sneered the man she'd stabbed. He was evidently healed and back to work. "Alone at last."

Heather's stomach flipped, but she straightened her spine, her notebook clasped firmly beneath one arm as she palmed her dirk in the other.

"We should grab 'er, an' make 'er pay fer stabbin' ye, eh wot?" another returned.

The healed man took a step forward, his eyebrow lifting when he caught sight of the dirk clutched in her hand. "We've 'eard ye screamin' yer pleasure fer th' cap'n. Why not let us show ye how well we can—"

"Say one more word, and I'll gut you," Heather warned. "And this time, you shan't heal from it."

With a wary glance at her weapon, the three men withdrew.

It was a disappointment that she couldn't win the good favour and loyalty of the crew without also giving them leave of her body. Such was fine, she supposed, as she would be free of them soon. But knowing that they had *heard* her... A shiver raced down her spine.

Pressing the latch to the captain's cabin, she opened the door and hurried into the darkness. She set her mother's notebook upon the table and went to her plants. They were flourishing in these conditions—bright sunlight for part of the day and plenty of fresh water when they required it.

She glanced out the window and saw naught but her moonlit reflection. The time had gotten away from her while she visited Duncan. It was growing late.

"How are you, darlings?" she asked her plants, crouching beside the little clump of roped-together pots.

She touched the leaves and tested the soil with her fingertips, then hummed. Some were too dry. "You're thirsty today. I shall get you some water."

Her mind worked as she looked after her plants. If they were to soon reach a pirate port, she didn't trust the men left aboard to not touch her things. And while they mightn't be interested in her plants, they would no doubt find *much* of interest hidden within the pages of her mother's journal. The thought made her uneasy.

All at once, an idea formulated in her mind, and she set about gathering the pilfered documents and various items for sewing. Mayhap it was ill-advised, but in that moment, it felt like the correct course.

She sat at the grand table and removed a boot, angling herself toward the wall of windows so she could see in the milky darkness. With careful precision, she used her dirk to open the inner lining of the cuff. It took a few minutes of squinting and some cautious knife work to cut a section of stitches wide enough, but soon she was able to slip the folded documents inside. All that was left was to close the seam neatly enough that no one would notice anything amiss if her boots were somehow examined.

CHAPTER 16

One more night. Percy's hands balled into fists at his side as he surveyed the crew through the growing darkness. On the morrow, they would reach the *Golfo Mexicano* and their port at San Luis. While he and Heather would still share each other's company on the journey home, they would by no means have the privacy of the captain's quarters. They were not even guaranteed a sodding officer's cabin. And that meant one more night alone with Heather, ensconced in their cabin.

There was no way to know how they would travel on the journey back to England, but one thing was certain: he couldn't lose what he'd developed with Heather. With every storm, discussion, meal, sparring session, and certainly every fuck, a part of him grew more attached to her presence.

It would be sodding difficult to let her go once they reached England. But the devil knew he must.

As though manifesting from his thoughts, Heather appeared at the quarterdeck's companionway and sauntered toward him.

"Good evening," he said as she neared.

"Good evening to *you*." She grinned at him, her gaze dipping to the opened neck of his greying shirt, then down to his tight black breeches, and back up.

Hell, but it put fire in his blood when she looked at him like that. And he'd had her only hours before.

To his relief, she turned to stand at his side and observed the crew with him. She cast a wary glance at the lanterns swaying with the ship's movements and shifted closer.

"I haven't been on the quarterdeck on a clear night," she noted. "How do you see?"

He followed her gaze into the obscurity beyond the bulwark. It was black as pitch, the lights from the lanterns doing nothing to minimize the darkness past the quarterdeck.

"It's like we're stationary," Heather whispered. "Floating in nothingness."

Percy nodded. "It is. It can be disorienting."

They stood thusly for countless moments while the pirates continued with their duties around them. The sea was calm, the air warm and filled with the salty scent of the sea. And flowers and earth. *Christ*, but the woman beside him always managed to fill his senses with her intoxicating love for plants. It was...disarming.

She gasped, and he blinked, returning to the moment. The light dusting of clouds above them parted to reveal a sky swathed in condensed waves of tiny stars. He'd seen the sight countless times in his life, but this view wasn't available in London, where the air was thick with coal smoke. When was the last time Heather had been to the English countryside and had seen the sky beyond London's chimneys?

He watched a faint flush of pleasure creep up her neck as she stared in awe. It must have been some time, indeed.

Heather's eyes glittered as she stared, as though trying to take it all in. Percy wished that the moment could stretch on indefinitely.

His gut abruptly twisted at the notion of pirate life grabbing hold. And, once again, concern for their future stole into his thoughts. His chest tightened. Why did their return to England—and he *would* return, damn it—mean the end for them? He couldn't marry her—that much was certain—but was it possible for them to continue their *affaire* until she found a man with whom she could have children and live out her best life?

That thought sent another pang through him, and he ground his teeth.

After all he'd done in his life, he didn't deserve even the quiet years he'd intended for himself. While he could not change what he'd been born into, there were moments, during his years of piracy, in which he'd truly enjoyed himself. Which was precisely why he was unfit to be a husband. He was damaged. It was not about only his name, birth, or experience. His very heart was...*soiled*. Regardless of what he wanted out of life—his peaceful apartments, his comfortable routine of a job, and time with friends—he was unworthy. And he'd best remember that.

He swallowed against the thickness that had settled in his throat.

A yawn escaped her, and he took her hand.

"Come," he urged, noting Donovan's arrival on the quarterdeck. "Let us go below. Tomorrow is no doubt to be an eventful day."

"AND HOW DOES a salve differ from a poultice, liniment, or herbal oil?" Percy asked, his gaze interested.

Heather swallowed her mouthful of chicken. The cook had certainly outdone himself with this meal, though the thought was decidedly morbid when coupled with the distinct lack of *cluck-cluck*ing from beyond their door.

"It's not terribly different from an herbal oil," she replied, feeling her passion for the topic flood her. "In fact, herbal oil must be used in the recipe."

Percy's dark brows lifted. "Indeed?"

"Yes. It is simply a combination of herbal oil, olive oil, and beeswax. One can rub it into the skin and receive all the benefits of the herbal oil without so much mess. It merely depends on what method of application you desire."

His lips pulled sideways in a half grin, his gaze intent on hers. "Fascinating."

"Whereas, as you know, liniments are strained liquids made from herbs and vinegar, and a poultice is simply crushed herbs and hot water, applied with strips of muslin." She sighed. "It is all so engrossing."

Percy nodded, cutting his chicken. "And have you decided to convert one of your new herbal oils into a salve?"

"I have. Duncan aided me in converting the catnip-and-fennel oil this afternoon. It is meant to settle one's stomach."

He blinked. "Do you *eat* it?"

Heather snorted. "I'm told one ought to rub the salve on their stomach, though they might wish to add some on their upper lip if they find the aroma pleasing."

"Mmm." He winked playfully. "It should prove useful if you experience seasickness again."

She laughed. "Indeed, it should."

"I saw yesterday that you'd done some research with the maps on the table. Were you able to discover any genus of plant that you wish to seek once we drop anchor in San Luis?"

Her eyes widened as another jolt of anticipation raced through her. "Yes, as it happens, I was."

They continued talking as they concluded their meal. Heather wasn't entirely certain that Percy was as interested in plants as he seemed, but she very much enjoyed sharing her newfound knowledge with him. In turn, he told her about navigation and what he knew about sailing.

At long last, he stood and held out his hand. Heather accepted, covering a yawn with her free hand. As though through silent agreement, they said nothing as they prepared for bed. And when she slipped between the bedclothes and lay on her side with Percy at her back, she had a sinking feeling of finality. She didn't want this to be their last night like this.

THE SUN ROSE EARLY the next morning—or at least it felt that way to Heather. She reached a hand out beside her, but the bedclothes were crisp and cool beneath her fingers. Her stomach swooped unpleasantly. Percy had left already.

It was an unrealistic hope to share intimacies one last time before they reached San Luis, but her body didn't seem to understand that.

The ship was eerily quiet. The creak of the wood, the splash of water, and the faint animal noises coming from beyond the cabin's door were the only sounds to be heard. A shiver of unease travelled up her spine, propelling her from the bed and quickly through her ablutions. Whatever was happening, it didn't feel good.

She donned her freshly cleaned and dried breeches, shirt, stockings, and stays, then slipped her feet into her boots and fastened her belt and sheath around her hips. Her stomach gave a little wobble, but she stood firm against it. It was time to face whatever the day held.

Without another moment's hesitation, she quit the cabin and ascended the companionway to the quarterdeck.

She emerged into utter stillness. All the pirates abovedecks stood mute, their gazes locked on their surroundings.

Heather spotted Percy near the bowsprit and strode toward him.

"What is happening?" she whispered as she drew close.

He smiled grimly, but pressed his lips to her ear. "We've reached *Golfo Mexicano*. These waters are full of other pirates —and British warships *searching* for pirates. We must sail with caution."

Heather trained her gaze ahead. Caution, indeed.

Minutes seemed to crawl by, the air filled with tension, perspiration, and the odd shuffling of feet on the creaky ship.

The silhouette of a ship appeared in the distance, and Heather held her breath. They moved swiftly on the water's surface, drawing nearer.

"It's not making to approach," Percy murmured in her ear.

Then, land was on the horizon, with other ships dotting the water around it. And suddenly, the tension began to melt away, replaced by a tangible excitement from the crew.

How long had it been since these men had seen land? Longer than Heather, no doubt, and yet she couldn't deny the buzz of anticipation that hummed just beneath her skin.

They approached quickly, sailing between moored ships before Percy finally began shouting orders.

"*Uncat the anchor*!" he bellowed. "We're here, men!"

THE ROWING BOAT rocked precariously as Percy helped Heather onto the dock, and his gut dipped with nerves. The sunlight brightened her hair, lending it hints of copper, and the warmth of the morning brought a rosy hue to her cheeks. She'd tied her hair in a knot at her crown—as she was wont to do—and some strands had broken free to frame her face. He wanted to run them through his fingers.

Instead, he winked at her as he tied off the boat. "Best to remain near to my side. Keep your dirk close to hand. Remember your training. And do not make eye contact with anyone unsavoury."

She glanced beyond the docks toward the pubs, shops, and brothels. "Percy, that is *everyone*."

He jerked his head in a nod. "We are in accord, then. Come. Donovan is to oversee the unloading of our pilfered goods. Let us find a ship bound for England."

He'd told the men to enjoy some recreation time, but they know naught of his intention to abandon them. Not even Donovan was aware of this plan.

He led the way from the docks into town. Heather fell into step beside him. She kept her hand draped easily over the sheath of her dirk, and her spine was stiff with the tension that veritably radiated off her.

Over the next hour, Percy approached at least a half-dozen first mates from different ships, and each looked at him as though he were mad. At their response, he'd followed up with inquiries about a possible vessel for purchase. Lord knew he could find men willing to make the journey for some coin, if he but had a means of transport.

"I daresay these men feel the same way that you did about approaching the shores of England in a pirate ship," Heather said, squinting toward town as they walked.

The gentle splash of seawater against the wood posts of the dock, the squawk of gulls, and the rhythmic thump of their boots hitting the planks echoed around them. All while his insides churned.

Percy grunted his agreement. He ought to have considered that before they arrived. And why he thought a merchant ship might be waiting in San Luis to bring them home was beyond him.

"I need to think," he muttered. "I *will* get you home, Heather. I simply need to consider all our options."

They reached the edge of town and passed a bo's'n and smithy before Heather spoke again.

"What if the officers aboard the British warships—and on the shores of England—did not *know* that a pirate ship was, in fact, a pirate ship?"

"How—" Percy frowned. "Do you mean we *hide* it?"

She shook her head, dislodging another lock of her golden-red hair. "No. I mean we *disguise* it."

"Most naval officers and captains are aware of all of England's sailing vessels. I doubt we could disguise the *Pandora* in any such manner so as to convince them it's one of theirs."

"What of a Spanish frigate? Or mayhap a merchant ship? There must be some ships that are not as well-known to English officers. Surely there is paint in San Luis for the figurehead, a new flag, and sensible attire that a sailor might wear for the crew."

"A merchant ship from the Americas, mayhap," Percy mused.

"Certainly! But..." She frowned with concern. "Have we the funds to purchase those items?"

"Of course." He lowered his voice and leaned closer so as not to be overheard. "Butcher left an abundance of coin on the *Pandora*, and the hold was full of pilfered goods that Donovan is selling today. As the captain, I receive a portion of those sales. Funds will not be an obstacle."

"Excellent. Then the challenge would be convincing the men to make the journey and engage in the farce. Maybe you could offer them the choice to remain here and join another crew? Or they can join us. The *Pandora* and her crew need remain in the Pool of London only long enough for us to disembark with our things."

Percy's pulse picked up speed as he considered the option. It could work. If they were to sufficiently disguise the *Pandora* and the men, they could disembark, and the *Pandora* could sail away before anyone was the wiser.

"I believe you've just solved our predicament with that brilliant mind of yours, Heather." He grinned at her. "We'll see you home yet."

She returned his smile, squinting up at him through the sunlight. "When shall we begin?"

"Immediately, I daresay. The crew will unquestionably spend the afternoon and evening carousing at the brothels and pubs, so we shall reconnect with Donovan on the morrow to discuss our plans. For the moment, you and I must do some shopping."

A SHIVER of unease travelled up Heather's spine as they strode along the darkened, wood-planked sidewalk of San Luis. The sun was setting, lending orange and pink hues to the sky. But they were walking among the shadows, between roughly constructed buildings with missing chunks of wall and holes in every roof.

A sharp twinge raced along Heather's ankle, and she hid a wince. They'd been walking all afternoon, and at some point, between purchasing a new flag and ordering clothing for the pirates, she had twisted her ankle on the boardwalk. She was well, of course, but the dratted uneven boards of the walk made her continuously miss her footing. Of course, her clumsiness was also due, in part, to her being entirely unused to walking on land.

"Here," Percy said softly. "This inn will do."

Heather followed his gaze to the building before them. Light shone from around the crooked door, slats were missing from the roof, and the entire building tilted ever so slightly to the left. "Why do we not return to the ship?"

"We've walked too far, I'm afraid," Percy replied with a shrug. "We could easily make the journey, but with nightfall imminent, we would undoubtedly be attacked. And while I don't doubt your ability to defend yourself, it might be best to bed down rather than risk injury."

Her ankle gave a timely throb, and Heather nodded. "Very well."

Stiffening her spine and tightening her grip on her dirk's handle at her hip, they entered the inn's taproom. Loud laughter and a bawdy shanty reached her ears first, before the overwhelming scent of body odour, ale, perfume, and urine assailed her nose and brought tears to her eyes.

"Blimey," she whispered.

Percy nodded and gripped her elbow, guiding her toward the innkeeper.

"Good evening, sir," Percy began. "I require a room."

The innkeeper's bleary, reddened gaze looked them both up and down, and his lip curled in a sneer. "How many hours ye be wanting?" he asked in a thick West Country accent.

"The night," Percy replied brusquely.

The innkeeper's brows lifted, and he shook his head. "I'd say yer a mite too auspicious, but 'oo am I t' say?" He tossed a set of keys on the rough wooden countertop. "Room's yers. Top floor, first door on yer left."

Percy touched his index finger to his eyebrow in a mock salute and tossed some coins on the counter before taking up the keys.

Another shiver raced up Heather's spine as she watched Percy move. Law, but he was as lithe as a wildcat hunting its prey and just as dangerous. She wanted him again, but... She sighed internally. Oughtn't they discuss...*this*, whatever it was? There were scant weeks until they reached London, and she didn't want it to end. They'd spent so much time discussing their interests, and yet she still felt as though she didn't know enough about him. What were his hopes for the future? Did he see her there?

Realization hit so suddenly that her stance faltered. The truth of it was, *she* saw *him* in *her* future.

"If'n I live an' breathe!" a voice shout-whispered in awe. "It's Percival! I thought ye *died*!"

Heather's skin prickled in a wave of gooseflesh as silence fell over the room and every gaze turned toward Percy. Some of the men looked fearful, others awestruck, and one or two seemed utterly gleeful.

Of course. With the events of the past weeks, she'd entirely forgotten that many pirates on Butcher's ship had also recognized Percival Baxter. And yet, in all their time together, she'd not questioned it. Nor had he offered information.

Who *was* Percy?

CHAPTER 17

*P*ulse drumming painfully against his ribs, Percy took in the faces of the men in the taproom. He'd known there would be seafaring men around, but he hadn't anticipated being noticed without his tattoos visible. What could he do now?

"Aye, I'm Percival," he confirmed, gripping Heather's hand and leading her between the tables toward the stairs.

"You fought in the battle of Dunsmere," one man slurred in awe.

"Aye," Percy grunted.

Another man stumbled forward. "I 'eard all th' men wot tried t' leave Butcher's crew was killed."

Fuck. Percy's lips thinned. "At least one man didn't."

Out of the corner of his eye, he saw Heather's gaze swing toward him. A muscle twitched in his jaw as he hid a wince.

"'Ow do we know it's 'im, then?" a new voice asked. "Lemme see yer tattoos!"

"It's 'im," the other man replied. "Y' can tell…"

The voices faded away as he rounded the corner with Heather, and they started up the stairs. His pulse thundered in his ears, nearly drowning out his aggravated breathing and the creak of the inn's wooden stairs.

The air grew increasingly dense with grease and heat with each floor they climbed. At last, they reached the top and closed themselves in their room.

It was precisely as he'd expected: peeling wallpaper, rough-hewn furniture set strategically about the small space, and—*Christ*, did he just see a mouse dart into the corner of the room? The air stank of sex and perfume. It was positively nauseating.

"Who are you to them, Percy?" Heather asked, whirling on him.

Percy leaned back against the door.

This was it, the end of any association she would have with him. He closed his eyes against the hurt and betrayal he was sure to see on her face. "Despite the public's knowledge of my chosen name of Percival Baxter, these men also know me as Percival MacDonald," he began, his throat tight. "Adopted son of Benjamin MacDonald, known as Butcher."

Heather gasped, and there was a shift of fabric, but Percy refused to look. "As you know, I was born and raised on the sea." He swallowed past the bile in his throat. "Ben—Butcher —claimed me as his own. Said that while I resembled my mother, my spirit matched his."

He cringed and pushed off the door, striding deeper into the diminutive bedchamber.

"Percy," Heather said softly, a hint of pity in her voice.

Pity. Bah! Of course she didn't pity him. She ought to be aghast at ever having spoken to him, let alone having allowed him liberties...

He raked a hand through his hair. *Hell's tits*.

"You are not like Butcher," she said.

"*But I am!*" He rounded on her, his cheeks hot and his gut knotted with shame.

She shook her head. "I know you, Percy—"

"No, you don't," he spat. "I was a pirate on Butcher's crew, Heather. Do you not know what that means?"

Her lips thinned, and her eyebrows curved upward in a look of combined pity and pleading. Percy had to look away, focusing instead on the darkness beyond the window.

"I know that you feel guilt, and that you attempted to change your life for the better. That you dedicate much of your time to helping others. That your best friend, Leo, adores and trusts you, and that you faced imprisonment and death to help *me*." The air stirred around him as she stepped closer, and he breathed in her floral, earthy scent. "You did nothing more than what you were raised to do. And then you got out... How *did* you escape Butcher?"

"I leapt from a gun port as we sailed away from Barataria Bay—not far from here, in fact—and swam ashore. There, I changed my name, joined another crew, and then another, and another, captaining numerous pirate crews. Despite my change in name, word spread of my apparent lineage. It wasn't long before *Percival Baxter* became just as notorious as *Percival MacDonald*.

"One day, I found myself on a privateer ship, where I met Leo. The privateers embraced me as one of their crew. Eventually, we were permitted to remain in England, though I daresay that is in large part due to Leo." He sighed, sitting on the foot of the bed.

Deep self-loathing and despair churned through Percy. The truth was out. Now Heather would turn away from him in abhorrence.

His heart gave a hard *thwump*. He felt ill. Couldn't bear the thought of her looking at him differently, of her hating him. *Fuck*.

She deserved so much better than him. Despite her already being ruined in the eyes of the *haut ton*, she could still find a good man who would give her the marriage, children, and large home that she probably wanted—that she deserved, *damn it.*

"No matter what happened in the past," she said, stepping between his legs and sifting her fingers through his dark hair, "you are not what he tried to make you. If you were, you would not have cared to escape."

He hesitated. "But...I killed him. If I were so different, I might have—"

"No." She gave a swift shake of her head. "You oughtn't think that way. Your actions *saved* us that day. You said it yourself: Butcher would have seen the entire crew murdered."

While that might be true, he would forevermore be a man who killed his father.

Unable to let her go just yet, he wrapped his arms around her hips, pulling her against him and rubbing his temple into her abdomen. "I'm sorry."

She was warm and *alive*. And comforting beyond reason.

"Shh," Heather hushed, continuing to comb her fingers through his hair. "There is nothing for which you need apologize to me, Percy."

He pulled back and met her gaze, his heart in his throat. "I'm not a good man, Heather. I withheld the truth from you, from Grace, Juliana, and Maria. I...I was not raised in a home with a family. Before befriending Leo and becoming his valet, I..." His throat bobbed, and he took a deep breath, steeling himself for the inevitable—and regrettable—pain he would cause her. "Whatever my future, I *will not* intentionally bring a child into this world."

Her eyes widened. "You don't want children?"

Percy winced. "I'm afraid not. Just the thought of furthering Butcher's bloodline veritably curdles my blo—"

She kissed him fast and hard, her tongue dancing with his, before she pulled back.

"I don't want children either," she confessed.

Hope wove around his heart. "Truly?"

She grinned. "Truly. But you must know that even if I *did* desire children—which I decidedly do not—there is nothing wrong with your blood. I like you just as you are—especially your pirate blood."

Despite himself, the heated prickle of tears threatened behind his eyes. *She likes me as I am*, he marvelled. *And she doesn't want children.* His heart gave another *thwump*, but this time in elation.

He matched her grin, and she kissed him again.

Percy came alive at the touch of her lips. He didn't deserve to feel so good, but he was just selfish enough to accept what she offered, to the devil with the consequences.

They moved quickly, disrobing and tossing articles of clothing about until they stood nude, wrapped in each other's arms. Percy's body ached with need, his cock already leaking, begging to be buried in Heather's sweet cunny.

HEATHER'S entire body fizzed with anticipation, and desire pooled low in her belly. She knew what pleasures intimacies with Percy would bring, and she could scarcely wait. The man not only kindled her desire but touched her heart. And she wanted nothing more than to feel all of him. Immediately.

"How would you like me?" she asked, tracing her fingertips along his tattoos, his skin hot beneath her touch.

He cupped her large arse and squeezed, groaning. "I want to fuck you fast and spend my seed on your glorious breasts. Then I want to sleep for an hour and do it all again."

"Yes." Heather nodded, her insides melting as a shiver wracked her frame. The contrast between his heat and the cooling air of the room added to the delicious sensations his words wrought. "Let's do that, please."

With the flash of a grin, Percy lifted her against him and deposited her on the bed.

"I won't take my time," he said, settling himself over her.

The heat of him, his beautiful heart, and his filthy words all made her core throb with need.

"I don't want you to," she breathed. "I want it as swift and hard as you can go."

He winked at her. "Whatever you desire, sweetheart. But first, you come."

Slicking the tip of his cock on her wetness, he used it to tease her, circling and circling, sending waves of throbbing, tingling pleasure through her. Her legs began to tremble, and a moan escaped between her panting breaths.

"Yes," Percy growled. "You're so good, so ready."

He bent forward to take one of her nipples into his mouth, and she cried out at the sudden jolt of pleasure, clutching him to her.

"Oh, Percy!"

He rolled the sensitive bud between his teeth before he moved on to the other. She arched her back, pressing herself eagerly into him and silently urging him to take more.

The delicious swirling and circling continued, the head of his erection an ideal combination of velvet and friction. Her pulse raced, her breathing turned ragged, and the coiling pleasure wound tighter and tighter.

"Percy, I'm going to—"

He groaned, leaving her breast to trail his lips along her collarbone and the side of her neck. "Come for me, sweetheart."

All at once, her back arched, and her inner muscles throbbed in time with her climax.

"*Fuck*," Percy growled.

If he were a wagering man, he would say that he'd never wanted a woman more than he did right now. But the devil knew he felt that way every time he was with Heather. Hell, but his cods were drawn up so tightly he was ready to spend right then.

But not before he'd been inside her.

"*Percy*," she gasped, tightening her hold on him.

Taking that as his cue, he lined himself up with her cunny and slid effortlessly inside her heat.

"My god, sweetheart."

He had to move slowly, to savour every bit of being inside her, skin to skin.

Without the condom, he felt *everything*. And he hadn't felt everything since their tryst in the gazebo, when this journey had begun. Fuck, he wouldn't change it for anything.

"I want it hard," she urged, wrapping her legs around his hips.

Christ, but he couldn't resist her wants. Withdrawing almost entirely, he snapped his hips back, thrusting deep and earning a cry and a full-body shudder from Heather.

Yes, like that. The room was filled with their panting, their moaning, and the rough slapping of their bodies. And he fucking loved it.

Again and again, he pumped his hips, thrusting deep inside her, until the telltale tingling rippled down his spine and into his ballocks. With a grunt, he pulled out, rose up on his knees, and shuffled forward until he was straddling her hips.

"Please," he begged. "Please stroke me, Heather."

Her green gaze glinted with power and desire as she closed her hand around his girth. She watched him carefully as she stroked, faster and tighter with each pass.

"*Fuck. Yes,*" he hissed, fists clenching at his sides and eyelids drooping as he watched her work.

Heather bit her lip. "Will you permit me to touch your—"

"Yes," he replied urgently, cutting her off. "You may touch me anywhere. *Everywhere.* Please."

Reaching with her other hand, he anticipated a caress to his cods, but she went past them to graze the crease of his arse. He couldn't help it. Just the thought of her willingly fucking his arse with her fingers sent him over the edge.

In a sudden burst of pleasure, his body stiffened, a hoarse shout ripped from his throat, and ropes of hot spend landed on Heather's breasts and belly.

Percy sighed, shivered, and slumped upon the bed next to her. "You are especially beautiful with my spend all over you," he said.

She laughed. "What a barbaric notion."

Turning on his side, he propped his head in one hand and looked down at her. "It's true, though. I...am growing rather addicted to being with you."

Hell, it was true. He didn't want to be parted from her once they reached England. Didn't want to give up the little world they'd created for themselves in the privacy of a bedchamber—or cabin, as it were.

Was it possible for them to continue a liaison when they returned and *not* be married? If he were to legally wed, she would be forced to take his legal name...*Butcher*'s name. And he couldn't have that. He didn't know if Heather would be receptive to being a mistress, but...could it work?

This couldn't be all it was for them, could it? *Neither* of them desired children—what a revelation!

Rising from the bed, he strode to the washbasin, wet a cloth with cool water and soap, and gave himself a cursory cleanse before bringing a fresh washcloth to Heather. He cleaned the seed from her skin, gooseflesh pebbling in the cloth's wake.

She clasped his hand, halting his progress. "I am, too. Growing addicted to being with you."

His heart hiccoughed, and he pressed a swift kiss to her lips before he tossed the cloth aside and lay on the bed with her. He reached for the bedclothes and covered their bodies before nestling against her with her back to his front.

It was time for sleep, but how could he? They were so near to their return journey to England...and there was so much more to say before they got there.

He pulled Heather tighter against his chest and pressed his nose into her hair. A smile tugged at his lips as he breathed in her warm, earthy scent. It was a marvel that she always smelled like plants, flowers, and earth, even when she'd been apart from her florae all day. His chest gave a pang. It was delightfully endearing. He loved hearing her talk all about the plants, their uses, and her intentions for the apothecary, even if he didn't understand half of it. The more her face lit up when she spoke of her passions, the more addicted he grew to hearing her.

Heather sighed and wiggled her arse against his satisfied cock, and he chuckled.

"Not ready yet, sweetheart."

She hummed, and Percy closed his eyes, letting warmth surround him.

Shouts echoed in the street beyond their window, disturbing their peaceful bubble. A frown pinched his brows. They were in San Luis with the devil knew how many pirates; there were bound to be duels fought and fights waged among the men.

More shouts rang out, and Heather sat up.

"What is happening?" she asked.

Percy patted the bed, still warm from her body. "Ignore it. It's likely just some men fighting about a wager or a woman."

She frowned. "Someone is issuing orders. Are they conducting a raid, do you suppose? Would they do that on a pirate island?"

Flicking the bedclothes aside, Heather retrieved her shirt and pulled it over her head as she padded toward the room's only window.

"There is no law here—"

She covered a gasp with both hands, dropping the window's curtain back in place.

Alarm jolted through him, and he hurried from the bed to her side. "What is it?"

"My god," she breathed behind her hands. "How did he find us?"

Percy peeled back the edge of the curtain with his index finger and looked down at the street below. The hairs on the back of his neck stood on end, and he uttered a low curse. The sodding Earl of Hanley had followed them to San Luis.

"WHAT ARE WE TO DO?" she asked, pacing before the foot of the bed. "Do you think he's learned of the pilfered documents?" She turned to face him. "He'll know that we're here. The men in the taproom recognized you—surely one of them will speak to the earl about our presence."

Percy nodded and reached for his breeches on the floor. "Get dressed as quickly as you can. We'll find a way out before they reach this floor."

With a nod, and her fingers trembling with trepidation, she found her own breeches and donned them. It took several heart-thudding moments for her to locate her belt and sheathed dirk, but she found them under the bed.

Boots, her inner voice whispered. Indeed, she could *not* forget those.

A commotion erupted belowstairs, the sounds of shouting voices and women's screams echoing up the stairs and through the narrow corridors.

Heather's heart lodged in her throat. "What do you suppose the earl's men are doing?"

Pausing in the act of sliding his arms into his coat-sleeves, Percy frowned. "Something doesn't feel right." He strode to the window and pulled back the curtain. "*Fuck.*"

Gut swooping, Heather hurried to his side. "What is it?"

People in various states of undress ran from the building, smoke billowing in their wake.

Heather's throat closed, and a shrill ringing began in her ears. *Fire.*

CHAPTER 18

"Heather." Percy put a hand to her shoulder. "*Heather*!"

She shook her head, her pulse fluttering.

Cursing, Percy moved about the room. There was a rattle and another curse.

This is it, Heather thought. They were going to die. She would never see her friends again, never be able to tell Percy just how much she'd come to care for him. The fire would claim them, just like a fire had claimed her parents.

Her mind's eye filled with memories of that horrid day—the charred skeleton of her childhood home, the scent of smoke permeating the air, the screams of her parents and the staff as they burned...

A shiver racked her frame, and tears prickled at her eyes.

"For fuck's sake, *Heather*!" Percy shouted, his face appearing before her, his hands clutching hers. "Do you not smell the smoke? We must *go*!"

She blinked, and he huffed a breath, turning on his heel and pulling her along with him toward the door. He tugged it open, and smoke billowed in.

Heather's throat all but closed up as terror seized her.

Percy cursed, then peered through the smoke-filled corridor. He coughed, closing the door again.

"The fire has reached our floor," he said urgently. "We must take the window."

We're going to die.

He turned and pulled her to the window, tugging the curtain aside and throwing up the sash.

"You don't mean f-for us to scale the side of the building, do you?" Heather asked, aghast.

"Just to the rooftop." Percy stuck his head out the window and looked up. "This roof connects to the next, and there are adequate footholds in the woodwork and the holes in the siding—"

"But how will we get down from the other roof?" Her voice had gone shrill with panic, but she could do little to contain it.

We're going to perish. You'll never make it home, her inner voice repeated. More people screamed, and Heather's heart constricted. *We can't make it.*

"Listen to me." Percy gripped her shoulders and brought his face to hers. "We're going to be fine, as long as we escape *now*."

Now. But the fire...

"*Now*, Heather."

BENDING out the window to peer up at the roof through the rapidly diminishing light, Percy swiftly mapped out potential routes in his mind before turning back to Heather.

He bit back another curse. She was fading in and out, one moment conscious of her surroundings, and the next lost in her panic. He'd seen this sort of terror, was fully aware of how dangerous it could be. And now was no different. He needed Heather to *focus*.

Smoke billowed through the cracks around the door, rapidly filling the air and growing denser toward the ceiling. If they didn't escape now, the air would become unbreathable, and they would, indeed, perish.

Worry churned in his stomach as he watched the emotions play over Heather's face. Evidently, she was afraid of fire. It would explain her desire to keep the lanterns unlit in his cabin. It was a fear, however, that they hadn't the time to politely navigate. He would have to take matters into his own hands, her feelings notwithstanding.

"I'm sorry, Heather, but we cannot prevaricate." Without another word, he lifted her in both hands and set her bottom on the sill. "Hold fast, here and here," he instructed, guiding her hands.

He reached after her, starting with one foot and securing a holding, before letting his body follow. The siding was dry and slightly crumbly, but it held his weight. Once he had entirely stepped out on the ledge, he guided Heather.

"Come along. Step just there," he urged. "That's right. Now step to that hole and test it with your weight."

She did as he bade, her fingers trembling and her breaths coming rapidly.

"You're doing so well," he said encouragingly, side-stepping along after her.

"There they are! Just there!" A shout rang out in the street below them.

Fuck. They'd been spotted.

Crack-thunk!

Heather screamed as the plaster next to her head exploded into dust.

Crack-thunk!

Jesus fuck, they're shooting at us. Percy's heart hiccoughed, and he reached out to Heather in an attempt to shield her.

"Don't shoot, you fool!" the Earl of Hanley's voice echoed. "She's no good to me dead. Go to that building. We'll cut them off on the ground."

Percy urged Heather upward, guiding each step, even while his heart beat a tattoo against his ribs.

"It'll be all right, Heather," he soothed, calling up to her. "You're doing so well."

Christ, but her movements were stiff and trembling.

"Only a few more steps."

She reached the roof's edge, and she hesitated. "I-I don't know if I can, Percy."

Smoke billowed around them and burned his lungs, but with effort, he kept his voice steady. "Grip the edge with one hand and place your foot just there in that hole, then lift. I will position myself beneath you and give your bottom a push and help keep you steady."

Heather hesitated again, but nodded. "I trust you."

Following his directions, Heather pulled herself up as Percy pushed her arse. It was a decidedly lovely handful, but this was not the time to ruminate on it.

At last, she scrambled up the roof, and a part of Percy's fear uncoiled.

He shadowed her movements, his muscles straining and a sweat breaking out across his brow. With one last heave, he pulled himself onto the roof.

"We made it," Heather breathed.

Striding closer on careful footing, Percy gripped Heather's hand in his. "Are you well, sweetheart?"

Her lips thinned, but she nodded again. "No, but I'm alive and with you, which is infinitely better than the alternative."

Percy lifted a brow. "Not quite. We must still escape this fire and flee your affianced."

"Very amusing, Percy," she grumbled.

He flashed her a grin and started off along the rooftop, her hand still clutched in his. The farther they traversed, the clearer the air became. But danger followed them. The earl's men were no doubt watching, waiting to strike the moment he and Heather attempted their descent.

So he urged her faster, racing along the row of weathered rooftops.

They were nearing the end when a loud crack rent the air, and the world fell out from beneath him.

CRACK!... Thunk!

In the span of one thunderous beat of Heather's heart, Percy was ripped from her grasp and gone in a cloud of dust and coal residue.

She skidded to a halt, her boots scraping along the roof slats. "*Percy!*"

There was a groan and a cough. "I'm well. The roof gave out."

She waved a hand in the air in an attempt to better see down the hole. *Blimey.* "Come, I'll help you up."

There was a shuffle of movement, and motion in the shadows, but she could scarcely see at all through the darkness.

"It might be simpler if you come down to me. We can exit through the building and hopefully misdirect the earl's men."

Shouts rose up in the distance, and her pulse jumped. "Yes," she urged. "Get me off this roof; I'm a veritable beacon up here."

Despite her instincts screaming at her to do otherwise, Heather approached the hole and crouched. *Creak.* She stepped back with a gasp.

"It's not sturdy," she said, her voice wavering. "How am I to sit over the edge when it is threatening to collapse?"

"Just drop down," he urged. "I'm here, ready to catch you."

She bit her lip. "*Drop*?"

"Yes. It's not as far down as you might think."

As foolish as this plan was, she trusted the man. So, her perspiring palms and quavering nerves notwithstanding, she lowered to her arse, slid to the edge of the hole, and dropped.

Whompf. Just as he'd said, Percy caught her with a grunt before setting her on her feet.

"There, now," he murmured, clasping her hand in his. "Safe. Are you well?"

Heather took stock of herself and smiled ruefully. "Trembling slightly, but a mite better than I was a quarter of an hour ago."

"Good. Let's find our way out of here."

Together, they navigated the dark attic rooms and descended the staircase. The floor boards creaked and groaned beneath their weight, the walls echoing back their rapid breathing and the clunks of their bootheels.

What was this place? Why was there no one around? Heather squinted through the darkness but couldn't identify anything around her. Where were the candles, the lanterns?

Percy led the way, but she hadn't the faintest idea how he could ascertain their direction. They descended two more narrow staircases and turned down a hall.

He stopped. "Fuck. We've hit a wall. This is the wrong way."

They spun around and carefully navigated another corridor before they reached the diminutive foyer. Relief loosened the knot in Heather's stomach, and she reached for the door.

"Don't," Percy whispered. "They might be out there. Allow me to check first."

The knot twisted tighter again, but she wouldn't allow fear to make her cower when she was capable of fighting. "I have my dirk. I can defend myself."

His lips thinned, but he nodded. "You are correct. We shall go together."

With a buoyancy in her heart that she hadn't expected to feel at his words, she opened the door. Beyond was a narrow dirt road with a wood-planked walking path on the opposite side. Smoke blew through the air, almost entirely covering the scent of the ocean.

"It's clear," Percy breathed. "Let's go."

Heather gave a nod and followed Percy onto the dirt road. Keeping to the shadows, they sped to the next building and pressed themselves against the door.

"*There they are!*" a man bellowed.

Percy cursed. "Run."

CHAPTER 19

Heather's lungs were afire. Her muscles ached, and her feet throbbed in time with her rapid pulse as she ran.

They wove around inebriated men and between rows of buildings, and yet footsteps still rang out behind them.

"I...can't go...much...further," Heather huffed out. "We will...have...to fight."

Percy led her around a sharp corner into a close, and stopped, forcing Heather to bump into his back. They crouched beside some piled crates.

"We must...catch our breath," he gasped.

Lanterns were lit at the end of the close, giving light to the soiled space around them. It was far from ideal, but preferable to being caught by the earl's men.

Rapid footfalls rushed past the close.

"I can't see 'em!" one voice said.

"They're around here somewhere," another replied. "Keep looking."

The voices faded, and Heather let out a deep breath.

Low, grating laughter echoed around them, and the hairs on the back of Heather's neck stood on end. *Who—*

"*No,*" Percy whispered, interrupting her thought.

The rosiness that had flooded his cheeks after their run abruptly fled, and his breath stuttered.

"Did ye think tha' ye could get rid of me?" the voice taunted. "Tha' ye could *steal* from *me?*"

Percy turned a fearful and urgent gaze to Heather. "I'm afraid we have to run again, sweetheart."

She nodded.

"Go. *Now.*"

Click.

Heather paused in the middle of her first step. That sound was unmistakable. It was a pistol being cocked.

"Ye took summat from me, Percival," he drawled. "So I shall take summat from *you.*"

"*No!*" Percy pressed his back to her, protecting her from the man.

Heather turned, peering over his shoulder at a hulking form with red hair, a grizzled grey-and-red beard, and horrific scars marring one side of his face. He had broad shoulders and a barrel chest, over which he wore...a bastardized Redcoat.

She gasped.

Butcher.

IT'S A GHOST. Percy's pulse raged through his body as horror washed over him.

Impossible. The man had survived. After all Percy's sodding confidence in his plan, it had failed bitterly. He'd thought the nightmare of Butcher was gone forever, but he was sorely mistaken.

"Tha's right," Butcher sneered, the pistol aimed at Percy's

chest never wavering. "I'm alive. Me own son betrayed me, like th' fucking coward 'e is. Couldnae even face me."

There was no time to think. He had to act.

Butcher scoffed. "And now th' bastard has nae words fer—"

Percy ran at the man, gripping his wrist and lifting.

Crack!

Blinding hot pain shot through the flesh of his arm, but he gritted his teeth against it as he fought with the enormous, muscular man.

"Percy!" Heather called. "You're—" She broke off with an echoing scream, and Percy's chest constricted.

"I got 'er, lads!" a voice said behind him.

"Bring her to the earl."

There was a scuffle behind him, even as he landed a blow to Butcher's gut.

"But I want to try her out first," one man said plaintively.

"Hanley's orders were—"

"Yes, I know, damn it."

There was a muffled shout before one of the men cried out in pain.

"The harridan *bit* me!"

"Take 'er blade."

There was more of a scuffle, and every nerve in Percy's body cried out for him to abandon Butcher and go to help Heather. But Butcher was more dangerous.

"Pick up 'er feet."

"But she's kicking! Christ, but she fights like a hellcat!"

The pistol clattered to the ground, and Percy slammed his forehead into the big man's nose. Butcher laughed, his blood-soaked teeth glinting in the lantern light, before a meaty fist slammed into Percy's jaw.

Blinding pain shot through his head, forcing him to blink away the blurriness.

The scuffling behind him began to fade, and his throat constricted. *Heather*. He couldn't let them leave with her.

In a quick succession of blows, he landed one to Butcher's throat, the injured side of his face, and his cods. But aside from soft grunts, the man showed no sign of injury.

"Ye forget, boy," Butcher sneered, "t'was I wot taught ye 'ow t' fight."

Fuck.

Percy went for the man's eyes, but Butcher side-stepped and jabbed Percy in the ribs. The wind left his lungs in a wheeze before Butcher leaned back and landed a flat-footed kick right to Percy's chest.

Pain lanced through him. And another blow knocked him flat on his back. *Air*. It was all he could think about. Not the pain, not the hot ooze of blood seeping from his head and tickling his scalp and arm. But *air*. He couldn't breathe.

Rapid throbbing pulsed throughout his body and fluttered with his erratic heartbeat. This was it. Heather had been taken, and he was going to die. He'd failed.

Butcher's grating laughter found its way past the rushing in his ears, just long enough for him to register the boot approaching his face. His world went dark.

IF THEY HAD BEEN brave enough and sought her out one at a time, Heather was certain that she could have defeated the earl's ruffian footmen and lent her aid to Percy. Instead, she'd watched as he fought for his life against Butcher, and Lord knew how that had gone.

Would Butcher keep Percy alive, or would he plan some sort of...torture? It was not to be borne.

She ought to have told Percy how she felt about him when

she'd had the chance. She ought to have *realized* how she felt about him, for pity's sake! But now it was too late.

He mightn't have returned her feelings, but while that would be painful, it hardly signified. She detested the thought of his going on with his life and not knowing how deeply she had come to love him.

Now, she sat in a chair at the table in the *America*'s wardroom with her wrists and ankles bound together, waiting for whatever punishment Hanley had planned for her. At least her hiding place for the documents had been successful, for one of Hanley's men had already conducted a cursory search of her person and missed them entirely.

Footfalls and shouts echoed about the frigate as they sailed away from the *Golfo Mexicano*, and Heather strained her eyes and ears, focusing beyond the doors.

The room, while almost entirely shrouded in darkness, was markedly similar to that of the *Sapphire*. A long, dark table stretched along the centre of the space, flanked by walls of white doors to the officers' cabins. It carried the scent of the sea and unwashed bodies, and the familiarity of it brought the threatening prickle of tears to her eyes. It reminded her of Percy.

One of the wardroom's doors swung open to admit two footmen and the earl, his spine slightly curved, his diaphanous skin pinkened—no doubt by the anger she saw flashing in his blue eyes—and his jaw clenched. In his hand, he carried a dangerously swinging oil lantern, and Heather's stomach dipped nauseatingly.

"I see that I gave you far too much leniency, Calluna." He set down the lantern and sat heavily in the chair at the table's head, his repulsed gaze sweeping her from head to booted foot. "We shall have to remedy that immediately. Just look at your hideous attire. It's entirely unbecoming."

The fluttering of nerves began in her abdomen, and her

chest constricted as both fear and anger battled for control over her emotions. "What do you intend to do with me?"

"I shall make you pay," he drawled. "Every day for the rest of your life."

A detestable crawling sensation washed over her skin, and she fought back a shiver.

One of the footmen standing guard behind the earl huffed a sneering laugh. He was one of the cowards who had apprehended her in San Luis, who had refused to face her alone.

"There is no getting away this time, Calluna," the earl continued.

Every day for the rest of your life... The realization crashed down on her like a terra-cotta pot. The old shite still meant to marry her!

A wave of gooseflesh began on her calves and worked its way up until the hairs on her head stood on end and a deep hopelessness washed over her. This was the end. Her position on Bow Street was truly gone, Percy was at the mercy of the man who raised him, and her—

She choked back a sob. Her cherished plants and her mother's beloved notebook were gone. All was entirely lost.

The earl stepped closer, his gaze dark and laced with malice. "I believe you have something of mine."

CHAPTER 20

Agony roared through Percy's head as he slowly came awake. He was dimly aware of movement and voices around him, but he could scarcely focus through the pain.

Someone touched him gently before a sharp pinch jabbed him in the arm. He groaned.

"Nae much longer now," a voice said soothingly. "We're almost done 'ere."

Percy knew that voice, but the fuzziness in his mind prevented him from identifying it.

"Ye've lost a lot o' blood, Percival," the voice said again.

"I want 'im alive long enough fer 'im t' see the results of 'is insolence." This voice he knew: *Butcher*.

Percy's blood turned to ice in his veins.

"As y' wish, Butcher."

Something tugged on the bullet wound on his arm, and in a moment of clarity, he realized where he was: the surgeon's room. Duncan was stitching him up, surely. But why go to the bother of healing him when Butcher was sure to kill him anyway?

To torture you, his mind whispered.

Clearly, Butcher had reclaimed his ship and his crew. Percy was but a prisoner. *Fuck*. He'd lost. He'd lost sodding everything. Hell, even Heather's plants were forfeit, likely already tossed into the sea.

An ache settled deep in his chest. *Heather*. There'd been a moment, lying abed with her in his arms, when he'd thought that maybe they could be more than paramours, that she could be *his* in truth. For his feelings wouldn't be shaken, no matter how many times he'd told himself that it couldn't work due to his past...his blood.

But look at what had happened: his life of piracy had come back to haunt him, and she had paid the price alongside him. For if Butcher hadn't stopped them, Percy would have been able to get Heather safely away from the earl's men. Now she was trapped with a man from whom she'd stolen incriminating evidence. Fuck knew what the man would do to her...

Percy's heart squeezed painfully. He'd been charged with her protection, and he'd once again failed. He'd not even had the cods to confess his feelings for her...

A cavernous void of emotion opened behind his sternum and began to spread, the numbness both calming his pulse and bringing a biting sting to the backs of his eyes.

"Ah," Butcher drawled. "Ye're awake."

Percy squinted his eyes open to see the man who'd raised him, his blazing gaze belying his gratified grin.

"So glad tha' ye're able t' 'ear this," the man continued. "We're approaching yer whore's ship even now." He laughed, the sound grating along Percy's nerves. "Aye, ye'll get t' see me kill 'er afore I keelhaul ye."

THE EARL WHEEZED A LAUGH, and Heather blinked in an attempt to see him through the tears blurring her vision.

He sneered. "I will, of course, graciously take you back once you've handed over the stolen documents—*you thieving whore*—and you will have no other recourse but to accept. We shall be married directly upon our arrival to my uncle's estate, and I shall be lauded a hero."

Heather's gut twisted with fear, all while said documents burned a proverbial hole in the cuff of her left boot. "You *can't!*"

"Indeed I can." He rose from his seat, the chair scraping along the wooden planks of the deck. "But first, I must make certain that you are not carrying that pirate's bastard. You shall be examined by the ship's surgeon, and if he deems it necessary, we will await your courses before dropping anchor."

The air veritably froze in her lungs. *Examine.* Surely he didn't mean to have the surgeon look *down there*. But the triumphant gleam in the earl's eyes told her differently.

"Wait here, Calluna," he instructed. "The surgeon is occupied in the sick bay at the moment. I shall retrieve you shortly. It is almost time for evening tea."

With that, he retrieved his lantern and strode from the room, closing the door with a damning click.

Hot fury chased away the fear lingering in her heart. This was not the way it would be. She would not allow the man to order an examination of her body. It was not to be borne!

She must escape somehow. Jumping from the ship was an ill plan, but perhaps she could convince someone to lower a rowing boat to the water. She would need to steal a satchel with foodstuffs, and...she must somehow incapacitate the earl and his men.

A plan began to form in her mind as she bit and tugged at the knotted rope at her wrists. Her pulse sped as she considered her options. It was a terrifying risk, but it would be worth it if she could be free of the earl. While she intended to use embarrassment and fear to dissuade him from seeking her hand in marriage, there was naught she could do to deter his pursuit of her while she was in possession of his incriminating documents.

The knot came loose at last, and she slid her wrists free, then went to work on the knot at her ankles.

The wardroom was nearly dark as pitch, but once she was free, she found her way into one of the officers' cabins and felt for a hanging lantern. It bumped against her palm, and she hastily pulled it down. Flint and steel were slightly more challenging to locate, but she found them in a nearby metal box.

Her arms laden with the required items, she returned to the wardroom's table. She set the lantern down and, with trembling fingers, set to lighting it. The flint and steel sparked several times, the sudden *crack...crack...crack* echoing off the cabin doors. Perspiration broke out across her brow, and she worried her bottom lip as the minutes passed. *I'm running out of time!* At last, the steel struck the flint just so, and the spark landed upon the lantern's oil-dampened wick, lighting it with a bright little flame.

The sight made her heart stutter, and she hesitated, her gaze flicking toward the wardroom's door and back. The earl had no doubt posted a guard outside the door to ensure her compliance. *This* was her way out of the room. She *must* continue.

Without another moment's hesitation, she stepped back, squeezed her eyes tightly shut, and smashed the lantern upon the table.

Crash!

Lantern oil splashed the tabletop and splattered the surrounding chairs and floor, taking the fire with it. Heat and a blast of light instantly filled the room, and for a moment, her heart tripped with terror. But she tamped it down, backing away until her back pressed against the cabin doors.

Body poised, she inhaled deeply and let out an ear-splitting scream. "*Fire!*"

THE DOOR SLAMMED BEHIND BUTCHER, leaving Percy alone with Duncan, and Percy struggled to swallow his emotions down. Butcher had Heather in his sights. And if given even one opportunity to attack...or kill, he would take it. Percy couldn't allow that to happen.

Tingles of fear raced down his legs as impatience swelled in his chest. "How much longer?"

Duncan tutted. "Nae long now." He glanced at the closed door and continued in an undertone, "Most crew members still support ye, Percival. Butcher has nae many loyal men aboard, but those few 'ave a watchful eye on goings-on."

"Thank you, Duncan."

The surgeon gave a short nod and knotted a bandage around his upper left arm, his shirt having been torn away under the man's care. Percy sat up and blinked away a wave of dizziness.

"Y' just tell yer Heather tha' she made a friend." He patted Percy's arm. "Ach, but ye'll need a weapon." Turning, he searched some crates and withdrew a French cutlass, sharp along one end of the blade and pointed to a glinting tip. "Now, I advise ye t' get rest, lest ye pop a stitch or faint from blood loss. But I expect ye cannae do tha'. There are guards posted outside me door, aye. Get th' Butcher, Percival."

Mystified and overwhelmed by Duncan's sheer faith in him, Percy mumbled his gratitude and dropped to his feet from the surgeon's table. Pain lanced through his head and jolted through his arm, and he gritted his teeth.

It was time to stop this.

Cutlass at the ready, he swung the door wide and emerged.

The man to his right startled and lifted his arm to aim a blunderbuss at him. But Percy struck first. With deadly precision, Percy sliced and jabbed, felling the man to the aft platform floor with a guttural groan, his blood pooling around him.

There was a shift of fabric, and Percy turned to face the other man.

The man raised his hands. "'E was loyal to Butcher, Cap'n, but I ain't. Butcher killed many o' us o'er the years, and I ain't glad 'e's back."

Percy couldn't afford to have a man stab him from behind, but Duncan had said that many were still loyal to him. So he'd have to trust the man.

With a nod, he slipped to the companionway and silently ascended.

CHAPTER 21

The heat in the wardroom intensified, and dread prickled along Heather's nerves as she waited. Though her world seemed to slow to a crawl, she was certain it would be only moments before the room flooded not only with the earl's men, but also with officers and crew.

"*Fire*! Get the buckets!" an officer bellowed.

Men scrambled and shouted, and Heather stealthily slipped from the room and down the nearest companionway. Heart racing, she reached the aft platform and peered into the surgeon's room. *Empty*. She released a breath and darted inside.

The diversion had been a success, but now came the true challenge of ensuring that she reach the earl's tea before it was brought to him.

In her lessons, Duncan had spoken of a new herbalist named Samuel Thomson, who lived in the Americas. The man had espoused the use of *Lobelia inflata* as an emetic and claimed that was a useful cure for a number of ailments. But curing ailments was not why Heather wanted it.

She searched the wall of vials and jars and, at last, discovered a small vial that fit in the palm of her hand. Its barely legible label was tied around its neck with string.

Voices boomed above her head, and she jumped. *Better move.*

On silent feet, she crept from the room. The ringing of the bell reverberated through the ship, and more men shouted and stomped about. With fear still riding her, Heather took advantage of the chaos and scrambled up two decks to the gun deck. The shouting continued, but she had eyes for only one thing: the kettle upon the galley's stove.

To her relief—and amazement—the crew, who had organized a system of water retrieval and bucket-passing, paid her no heed as she slunk closer. The cook seemed intent on shutting down the oven's fires, so with speed and focused intent, Heather lunged toward the still-steaming kettle and poured the vial's contents down the spout.

"Where's the Earl of Hanley's tea?" one of the earl's footmen asked.

Heather quickly ducked behind a cask, deliberately slowing her breath so that she wouldn't be heard.

"Now's not the time for tea," the cook replied gruffly.

A crawling sensation raced up Heather's neck and she turned her gaze sideways. And froze. Berta stood nearby, a small bucket of water in-hand, and her gaze locked on Heather's.

Sodding hell. I've been caught.

"The earl has requested it," the man continued. "And if I don't have it—"

"Get it yourself," the cook interjected. "Water's already boiled, but I've got to shut it down."

Berta's gaze flicked toward the men, then back to Heather behind the cask. Berta's lips quirked and she gave a subtle nod before striding away. The maid wouldn't reveal the truth.

Relief swept through Heather, even while guilt shrouded her heart.

Behind her, there was a grumble and the clink of earthenware before footsteps shuffled away.

"To your stations!" someone shouted.

Heather backed away and darted up the companionway to the quarterdeck. Here was even more chaos, and for the first time, confusion marred her brow and worry crawled up her spine. Something wasn't right. Were these men *all* intent on fighting the fire? Had she done more than create a diversion?

"*Run out the cannons!*" the captain bellowed. "*Guns at the ready!*"

Heather's breath seized in her throat, and her gaze swung wildly aft. And there was Butcher at the bow of the *Pandora*, his light eyes wide and alight with triumph...and revenge.

WITH A THROATY GURGLE, the blighter slumped to the ground, dislodging himself from Percy's blade. Most men had ignored his ascent through the decks, but the men who had fought ended up dead.

A wave of dizziness stole over Percy, and he took a slow breath. He was almost there. He had to stop Butcher.

Boom! Boom-boom!

His insides twisted sickeningly. *The battle has begun.*

With renewed vigour, he dashed up the companionway to the quarterdeck. Gunpowder filled the air, and the men's voices carried as they shouted.

Butcher stood at the ship's bow, his spine stiff and shoulders back as he barked orders at the crew.

"*Fire!*"

Crack, crack-crack, crack! Boom! Boom... Boom!

Vibrations travelled up Percy's legs as his gaze followed the gunmen's fire and the carronades' balls. Some sailed over the other ship, but one crashed into the bulwark and another into the running rigging.

Men shouted and scrambled about, apparently unprepared for battle. *Fuck.*

Rapid footfalls came up behind Percy, and he spun, lifting his cutlass just in time to block a blow from one of Butcher's men.

Boom-boom! Boom!

A cannonball glanced off the splintered taffrail to hit a gunner's leg, then bounced across the deck. The man screeched.

His opponent took advantage of Percy's distraction and lunged, but Percy turned sideways, forcing the man's blade to scrape past his belt, rather than gut him. He blinked past the momentary dizziness that swam in his head and gritted his teeth against the throbbing pain to his injuries. He could do this. He *would* do this.

Stepping back, he entered the ready position and was gratified to see the slight hesitation in the pirate's gaze.

Crack-crack-crack-crack!

"*Keep firing*!" Butcher bellowed.

Boom!

The ship shook, but Percy was ready for it. With a narrow arc, his cutlass sliced through the air as he advanced, cutting shallowly into the man's skin. His opponent bellowed and retreated, holding his chest.

The shock and fear on the pirate's features turned swiftly into fury, and he charged.

Fuck. Percy sidestepped the man's blow and rounded on him in one fluid motion, impaling him through his side as he ran past. With a groan and a gurgle, the man was felled to the deck.

Boom, boom!

Just as soon as that pirate was defeated, another took his place, a dirk in each hand.

"You don't wish to fight me," Percy called to the man over the din.

"Aye, I do. Butcher brought us glory. An' women. An' 'e wants ye dead."

The man lunged.

Boom, boom-boom!

The low noise reverberated in Heather's ears, and ripples of fear travelled up her spine. She hadn't anticipated the battle, but she would have to make her plan work. Butcher would murder everyone on board, and she needed to find Percy and take him home to England. There *must* be a way.

"You," the Earl of Hanley growled from the companionway next to her. "How *dare* you start that fire! I know what you've done, Calluna, and you shan't get away with it. Come with me belowdecks *now*."

Heather retreated a step and shook her head. "No."

His face turned a deep shade of purple, and his mouth opened to speak, but Heather missed his words entirely when pirates from the *Pandora* swung from the fighting tops and ran across the wooden plank positioned between the two ships, swarming the *America*'s crew.

"*Now, Calluna!*" the earl shouted, his demeanour growing hysterical. Sweat gleamed on his brow and upper lip. "Give back what is mine, damn it!"

Boom! Boom-boom!

Movement to her left caught her notice, and she narrowly evaded a falling man. Following Percy's unintended lesson from all those days before, Heather crouched beside the felled man and divested him of his dirk and cutlass. Then she approached the Earl of Shite, aiming the blade of her cutlass at his throat.

"You shall *never* have me," she said, nerves and hope both twisting in her stomach. *This is it.* "In fact, you ought to *fear* me."

His chin trembled, and the sweat began to slide down his temples. "I shall never fear you."

"You think not?" She huffed a laugh of derision. "I do, in fact, have something of yours, Earl."

"I knew it. You *bitch*!" he hissed.

"I also gave something to you." She paused, allowing him a moment to feel her gift.

Boom-boom!

The earl's eyes grew wide, and his skin took on a decidedly green hue. "*What have you done to me?*"

Heather smirked. "How are you feeling?" She paused, as horror entered his eyes. "I know every herb and plant that can kill you swiftly, or slowly and painfully, and that is undetectable through taste or scent. No one would know how you'd perished."

"I say..." he quavered, his throat bobbing.

She stepped closer, her blade only a hair's breadth away from the thin skin of his jaw. "Your acts of high treason will soon be known by all of England, oh Earl of Shite. And if you dare attempt to harm me or mine...you'd best not eat or drink anything ever again."

"I always knew you were a right b—" His words were cut off as he pulled away and raced toward the bulwark to cast up his accounts into the sea.

Swift relief warmed her. That was the earl taken care of.

"Look-ee who we got 'ere."

Boom! Boom, boom!

Heather spun to see one of the pirates who'd accosted her

on the *Pandora*, his lips pulled back in a sneer and his eyes glazed with triumph.

"You have nothing," she returned.

"Th' cap'n wants 'er alive," another pirate interjected.

Despite the swoop of nerves in her abdomen, Heather entered the ready stance that Percy had taught her.

Crack-crack! Boom!

The first pirate laughed. "She'll still be alive when I'm done with 'er. Jus' enough fer th' cap'n t' kill 'er in front o' Percival."

Breath caught in her throat, and her ears were suddenly flooded with the drumming of her heart. *Percy. He's alive!*

Her gaze slid past the two approaching pirates to the *Pandora*, where she could clearly see Butcher in his Redcoat fighting some of the earl's men. There were others fighting on the *Pandora's* quarterdeck, and one man with a bandaged head and arm—

Joy warmed her chest, and she had to resist running through the battle to reach him. Instead, she raised her weapons.

"Oooh," the first pirate taunted with a sneer. "Think ye can use men's weapons? Yer outnumbered, wench, an' there's no one wot would save ye—"

She lunged, grazing his ribs with her cutlass as he leapt to the side, then spun, slicing his arm with her dirk. He bellowed and dropped his weapon, holding his arm where she'd cut him.

The second man made for an attack, but he halted abruptly, his face stunned, before he fell to the ground with a cutlass in his back.

And there stood Duncan, his beard windblown and glasses askew.

"I'm righ' pleased t' see ye, Heather." He grinned, before shoving aside a fighting trio. "I need ye t' know tha' yer flora are in th' hull o' th' *Pandora*, along with th' items ye purchased. D' ye ken?"

A sob ripped from her throat, and she rushed forward to pull the dear man into a hug. "Thank you, Duncan."

The plan could still work. If the items they'd purchased in San Luis had made it onto the ship, they could still return home. All she needed was Percy.

Boom! Boom-boom! Crack, crack!

"O' course, lass," Duncan murmured.

Pulling back, she caught his warm blue gaze. "Be careful." She squeezed his arm affectionately and darted into the chaos around them.

She wove between groups in battle, narrowly avoiding being hit by meaty fists and sharp blades. Blood splattered her breeches and boots, but she gave it little thought as she focused her attention on reaching the man she loved.

CHAPTER 22

*P*ulse racing and lungs labouring, Percy swung his cutlass at his opponent, finally making a deep slice in the cur and felling him to the quarterdeck boards.

He *must* reach Butcher, must prevent him from finding Heather.

Boom! Crack-crack!

The ship vibrated with every blast of the cannons and carronades, and each one was followed by a lacklustre splash or the splintering of wood. And screams. Always screams.

Urgency rushed him, and he scanned the deck. A flash of red caught his gaze. There Butcher was, marching through the throng, his gaze transfixed on a target. Percy followed the man's line of sight, and all at once both elation and terror slammed into his chest. *Heather*. Her eyes were just for Percy as she strode across the gangplank and onto the *Pandora*.

Boom-boom!

One of the *America*'s sails rent with a loud *rrrrrip*, but it scarcely registered. His pulse faltered.

The words "Look out!" were wrenched hoarsely from his

throat, only in time for her to turn and see Butcher's thick hand grip her around the throat.

Percy's heart all but stopped, and he ran toward them, shoving and kicking any man who happened into his way. He couldn't let Heather die. He *wouldn't*.

THE AIR SQUEEZED from Heather's throat and the blood rushed to her head as Butcher gripped her neck. Instant panic flared in her chest. The urge to pull at his hand and kick was overwhelming, but she forced herself to recall Percy's teachings.

Boom! Crack-crack-crack!

Her lips began to bulge, and her face was undoubtedly deep red, so without hesitation, she lifted her arms in the air to either side of his, and spun, swiftly bringing her inside elbow down on his forearm. The slide of his fingertips along her throat burned, but she gulped in a breath as soon as she was free.

Keeping her movement going, she turned again, thrusting her other hand out before her and connecting the heel of her palm to Butcher's blood-splattered nose. Cartilage and bone gave way with a sickening crunch.

Butcher bellowed, and yet more blood spurted from the appendage.

Boom-boom! Boom!

Heather blinked the last of the spots from her vision, satisfied that she'd shown her mettle, then drew her leg back to kick him in the ballocks. But he blocked it. With bloodied hands, he clasped her ankle and tugged, pulling her entirely off balance. She landed on her back, the air left her lungs with a whoosh, and her pulse stuttered.

He had her. This was it.

With a maniacal gleam in his eye and a smirk that tugged at the scars marring half his face, Butcher withdrew a dirk and held it aloft, prepared to slice down into her. Heather stiffened. The only way out was to roll, but to one side of her was the belfry and to the other, a cannon. Her vision wavered with terror.

But Butcher paused.

Heather blinked just as a blade was drawn across Butcher's throat. With a gasp, Heather shuffled backward as Butcher blinked, his eyes gone wide and mouth agape. Then, blood spilled forth.

Boom!

The man choked and sputtered, and, like a great tree falling in the forest, he crashed to the quarterdeck.

And there stood Percy, ashen and heaving. Heather couldn't have loved him more in that moment.

"*Heather.*" Percy wiped his cutlass on Butcher's back and stepped past him to rush to Heather's side, his body alight with conflicting concern and jubilation.

She accepted his proffered hand and staggered to her feet. "Thank you, Percy. I fear my skill at combat has not yet been mastered."

Christ, but her voice was hoarse. Percy's gaze slipped to the red marks around her neck, and he scowled, anger flaring to life once more in his chest.

Boom-boom-boom!

The ship shook, and he adjusted his footing, Heather's hand still clasped gently in his.

"Your abilities in combat are excellent. The man was simply able to withstand a great deal of pain." Percy caressed the back of her hand with the pad of his thumb as nerves prickled in his stomach. "There is no harm in continuing to practise...together." He cleared his throat. "Perhaps when we return home?"

"Of course, you must be right." She nodded, a half-smile tugging at her lips. "Continuing our training is a lovely idea. I'm sure Juliana and Maria would benefit from further instruction as well."

Hell's tits. Just say it, man.

"Y-yes, of course. That is t-to say," he stammered, the prickling of nerves growing into a full assault on his abdomen. "I...want more than that."

A gentle frown puckered her brow, and she stepped sideways, smoothly avoiding a fighting duo. "More? I'm not sure I understand."

Words failed him. He wanted *her*. All of her. He wanted a home and a marriage, devotion and trust. He wanted to be her family.

But the words wouldn't come. They were stuck in his chest as though readying to burst forth. So instead, he slid his fingertips along her jaw and swept forward to capture her lips with his. It was swift and sweet, but it sent heat through his body just the same.

Boom! Boom-Boom!

He pulled back to press his forehead to hers. "I've fallen in love with you, Heather."

"Have you?" Heather's cheeks flushed as she stared at him through wide eyes.

"I have."

She beamed, her face veritably lighting from within. "I love you as well, Percy."

Pleasure—and no small amount of relief—warmed his chest, and he returned her smile. "Then we have much to discuss. But first, shall we end this battle and begin the journey home?"

Her smile still in place, Heather nodded. "Indeed. I'm given to understand that the items we purchased are safely stored in the hull."

Christ, but that was fortunate. He'd thought they would have to briefly return to San Luis.

With another grin, he swept forward to buss her lips, then stepped back and turned to the belfry. He tugged the rope.

Bong...bong...bong...bong...

Three weeks later

HEART THUNDERING, Heather dismounted from Percy's lap to sidle up against him upon the gently swaying bed in the *Pandora*'s captain's cabin. Her rapid breaths ruffled the smattering of tight curls upon his chest, and she dazedly traced a finger along the anchor there.

Percy hugged her closer. "I'll never tire of that, love."

She huffed a laugh. "Neither shall I."

Percy had come to know her body so well that he knew just where to touch to elicit a response.

And the delights of her evenings alone with Percy had been a necessary reprieve from the flurry of activity these past weeks. Those crewmen who had agreed to their scheme and remained aboard had spent much of the time repairing and disguising the ship in preparation for the journey to London.

After the battle, they'd left the earl and the crew aboard the *America* to their own repairs, but Heather knew not of their intentions. Hanley hadn't an affianced with him to satisfy his cousin's whims, but he no doubt knew that if he returned to England, he would be apprehended and tried for high treason. It didn't feel right to simply let him flee, to allow him to create a life for himself in the Americas, but she would leave the chase to the Royal Navy.

She just wished she knew to which royal the earl had made his alliance, for she would do all in her power to take them down as well.

Percy sighed, patting her hand with his callused one. She looked up at his dear face, her pulse picking up speed once more.

"What of when we reach London?" she asked. "We are naught more than a sennight away now, surely. Will you live with me at the Bow Street offices?"

"Mmm," he hummed. "I'd thought to purchase a home for us in town, somewhere close enough to the offices that it will not be inconvenient to reach them every day."

"For *us*? Truly?"

He jerked his chin in a nod. "Truly. So long as you will have me." He hesitated briefly. "And I'd rather hoped that you would accept my hand and become my wife. But I understand if you are diffident toward marriage, so I would be glad to have you any way that I can, whether as a wife, a companion, or a paramour."

"Oh, Percy," she breathed. The answer was obvious to her, for she'd already begun to think of what she wanted out of her time with Percy. She had his love, and now she would have *him*. "Of course I shall marry you."

A SENNIGHT *later*

"*Row, row, row*..." The rhythmic voices of the men on the gun deck echoed up to Percy on the quarterdeck.

The remainder of the crew was still, as though holding

their collective breath as the *Pandora* sailed slowly down the River Thames, nearing the Pool of London. High above them, they flew the flag of a previously captured ship, *Briar's Thorn*. And the men had donned clean slops, brown or blue coats, and had cleaned their faces and hair. The ship had been cleaned and painted.

It was the best they could manage, and Percy hoped it worked. No one had stopped them yet, which was promising, but they had yet to drop anchor in the Pool.

Early morning light glittered on the rippling water of the Thames and reflected the blues, pinks, and oranges that streaked across the hazy London sky.

"Getting close now, sir," Donovan said, appearing at his side.

"Indeed," Percy grunted. "We've made it this far without detection, but we must remain alert."

"Aye, Captain."

Percy's gaze slid toward Heather at his other side, her hair knotted high on her crown and shining copper in the golden light. She looked every bit the lady she was, in the mauve morning dress that she'd reacquired from among her things on the *America*. Pride swelled inside him.

Never in his life would he have thought that he would ask a woman to be his wife. He'd always considered it impossible, not only due to his bastardy, but because he could never consign a woman to a future without the children that she likely desired. But Heather... She both loved him *for* his lineage and shared his desire for a childless future. She was utterly remarkable, unlike any woman he'd ever known. Hell, even the few women with whom he'd engaged in meaningless trysts had condemned his use of condoms and expressed a desire for a bairn.

Heather was his perfect partner. She was intelligent, amusing, kind, caring, and so sodding strong. And she would be his.

"Why are you smiling like that?" she asked, quirking one eyebrow.

Percy lifted her hand in his and pressed a kiss to the backs of her fingers. "Just thinking of you, love."

She huffed a breath. "You know I adore hearing that. But you really must focus on our arrival."

"So I ought."

"*Row...row...row...*" the chanting continued.

"*Starboard*," Percy shouted.

"*Starboard!*" the gun deck's bo's'n echoed.

They glided to the right and forward, officially entering the Pool of London. Percy's gut clenched, and a zing of apprehension went up the backs of his legs. He'd not be so worried if it were just *his* safety at stake, but it was the crew's as well... and it was Heather's.

Other ships were moored around them, dotting the water's surface. Men rowed to and from the ships in smaller boats and moved about the docks, numerous naval officers among them.

This is close enough.

"*Halt!*" Percy hollered, and the gun deck's bo's'n repeated. "Uncat the anchor!"

The crew did as they were told but remained carefully silent. It was almost eerie, but Percy understood their reticence to call attention to themselves. They simply needed to get Heather, her many plants, and Percy off the ship. And then they could sail away. Quickly.

"Lower the boats!" Percy called before he turned to Donovan. "The moment I set foot on that rowing boat, you're the captain. If you would, please see our things to shore and get yourselves safely out of England."

"Aye, Captain." Donovan grinned. "I imagine that some men might very well wish to bury their Jolly Roger for good. Afore we came across th' *Sapphire*, we found an island in the tropics at which many of the crew wanted to remain. But Butcher kept us moving in search of more riches an' glory. Mayhap we'll return."

Percy clapped him on the shoulder. "A capital idea, my friend." He paused. "Thank you, Donovan, for your support and your aid throughout this journey. It hasn't been easy, and the work you and the men have done has been appreciated."

The man's smile grew. "O' course, Percival. I'm glad to've gotten th' chance to see y' again."

"Likewise."

The ship slowed to a stop, and the rowing boats were lowered. The crew moved swiftly, bringing Heather's abundance of plants to one of the boats.

Percy retrieved his satchel, threw it over one shoulder, and extended his hand to Heather. "Are you ready to return home?"

She winked, accepting his proffered hand. "Aye, Captain."

EPILOGUE

A fortnight later

"Thank you, Bernard." Heather smiled to their butler as she and Percy strode from their house in town and onto the sidewalk.

"A pleasure, of course, Mrs. Baxter." He sketched a bow, still holding the door open with one hand. "Mr. Baxter."

A thrill of pleasure at hearing her married name raced up Heather's spine. They'd been married only five days, but she would surely never tire of it.

Percy tipped his hat with a grin and offered his elbow to Heather as they fell into step.

Heat from the sun warmed her through her smart green walking dress. The bodice was modest, and the sleeves cut at the elbow, despite the warmth of the midsummer morning. Percy had commissioned it—and numerous others—from Maria's brother Thomas upon their return to England.

Thomas was their office's costume designer and creator, and he was markedly talented in his craft.

Carriages rolled by, led by trotting horses and driven by yawning men. They lived on a busy lane—that grew busier as the morning went on—but the convenient walk to the Bow Street offices was not to be outdone.

"Are you looking forward to returning to work after so long?" Percy asked.

Heather smiled up at him, and her stomach swooped happily. He was incredibly handsome in his tailored fawn coat and breeches, a brown striped waistcoat that matched the precise shade of his eyes, a white shirt and cravat, and shining black Hessians.

"I am, indeed," she returned. "I'm given to understand that three more recruits have joined our ranks and require training."

His lips quirked. "So I've heard."

Anticipation bubbled beneath her skin. "I can scarcely wait to make their acquaintance. Grace has informed me that the women approached *her*, seeking employment." Heather bounced on her toes. "Word of our runner offices must have reached a great many people. I daresay we shall have an abundance of clients."

"I imagine we shall, love."

She beamed at him as they rounded the corner onto Bow Street.

Her pirate cut so fine a figure in his new attire that she struggled to look away from him. After they'd returned to England, Heather had fretted that he might miss his life at sea, but she'd come to learn that while he had once valued his friendships with those men, the thought of being pulled back into the life wrought fear in him.

She squeezed his arm affectionately as they approached the door to the offices. It swung open to reveal Miss Grace

Huntsbury, the woman who had founded their group of runners.

"Heather! Percy!" A dimple appeared on one of her cheeks. "Please come in. I had cook prepare the morning meal for us all in the dining room."

Heather leaned in to buss Grace's cheek. "How kind of you, dear."

They placed their hats on nearby hooks and preceded Grace past their parlour-turned-offices and through to the dining room. There sat Juliana and Leonard Notley, the Marchioness and Marquess of Livingston, Maria and Jasper Sinclair, the Duchess and Duke of Derby, Mr. Thomas Roberts—Maria's brother—and three beautiful, buxom women whom Heather didn't know.

Her friends swept forward in greeting, offering congratulations and warm embraces.

Heather's eyes stung, but she blinked the tears away. While she'd seen her friends at her wedding, they'd not had the opportunity to speak in depth. Now she wanted most fervently to speak with them, to discuss the past months and inquire about their lives. But they had new recruits in the room, and she didn't wish to be rude.

"My apologies," Heather said as she turned to the new women. "My name is Mrs. Heather Baxter, and this is my husband, Mr. Percy Baxter. Percy teaches combat in the rooms belowstairs, and I am a runner—like you."

"She is also soon to be to be our in-office apothecary," Grace announced with pride.

Heather's chest warmed. Indeed, she'd already begun to gather the necessary items to begin the new practice, and to populate the remarkable greenhouse that Percy had insisted he install in their new home. Her heart veritably bubbled over.

A woman with bright copper curls, pale skin, and brown eyes dipped in a shallow curtsey. "I am Mrs. Sophia Perry."

Heather opened her mouth to speak, but the next woman stepped forward and curtseyed as well. She had light blonde hair, a smattering of freckles across the bridge of her nose, and brilliant blue eyes.

"My name is Miss Phoebe Arnold."

"And I am Miss Edith Bartlett." A tall, dark-skinned woman with enchanting eyes flashed her a grin.

Heather smiled at the three women. "I am so pleased to make your acquaintance."

"Edith is also an apothecary," Grace said from her position at the table's head.

Anticipation zipped up Heather's spine, and her eyebrows shot up as she gazed with interest at the woman. "Are you, indeed? Do let's be seated. I believe that you and I will have a great deal to discuss."

TABLEWARE CLINKED, and a steady hum of voices surrounded Percy as they broke their fast. He was both relieved and glad to have returned home, and to have married the woman he'd come to love so dearly. His stomach gave a familiar happy wobble, and he hid a grin. He'd never known joy such as this.

Heather was remarkable. His gaze slid across the table to where she sat in deep conversation with Miss Edith Bartlett, no doubt discussing her abundance of plants and what they could do for the apothecary.

Pride swept over him. He could scarcely wait to see what their future held and what adventures they would have as she took on new clients. Life with Heather would never be dull.

Percy sipped on his coffee, relishing the earthy burn that stole down his throat.

"What—" Miss Huntsbury dropped her fork to the table as a maid raced in.

"Beggin' your pardon, but there's a woman 'ere wot says she needs 'elp."

She gestured behind her, and a petite woman with dark brown hair and red-rimmed hazel eyes entered.

"I'm ever so sorry to interrupt your morning meal. I can return—"

"Nonsense." Miss Huntsbury stood and helped the woman to her seat. "How can we help you?"

The woman dabbed at her reddened nose with a kerchief, her gaze hesitant as she took in the room. "Erm..." She straightened her shoulders and began again. "I need your help. My haberdashery is being threatened by the gentleman owner of the bookstore next door to my shop. And a notice came 'round this morning stating that I had all but eight-and-forty hours to vacate or I would be sent to gaol." Her eyes welled up with tears. "Please. Please help me."

Miss Huntsbury's lips thinned as she faced the women at the table. "Come, ladies. We have work to accomplish."

ABOUT THE AUTHOR

Award winning queer and autistic author of steamy and suspenseful historical romances. Cheri began writing as a child and fell in love with historical romance as an early teen. Finally, she combined her two passions and started writing heart-pounding historical romances full of danger, spice, and a guaranteed happily-ever-after.

She lives in BC, Canada with her high school sweetheart husband, their four neuro-spicy children, and their dogs. She/they.

Readers can find Cheri on TikTok, Instagram, Discord, Bluesky, Threads, Lemon8, and Rednote. Links are available on Cheri's Linktree via her website: www.cherichampagne.com.